To Jim

for

The Sixth

WILLIAM—THE DICTATOR

By the Same Author

"I'LL TAKE THAT UP," SAID WILLIAM, "SO'S TO SAVE YOU
TROUBLE."

(*See page* 127.)

WILLIAM—THE DICTATOR

BY

RICHMAL CROMPTON

ILLUSTRATED BY
THOMAS HENRY

LONDON
GEORGE NEWNES LIMITED
TOWER HOUSE, SOUTHAMPTON STREET
STRAND, W.C. 2

First Published	.	.	*June 1938*
Eighth Impression	.	.	.	*1947*
Ninth Impression	.	.	.	*1949*

Printed in Great Britain by
Wyman & Sons, Limited, London, Fakenham and Reading

CONTENTS

TO
DAVID (AGED 4)

CHAPTER I

HE WHO FIGHTS

IT was the summer holidays, and William was feeling a little bored. Ginger, Henry and Douglas, and indeed most of the junior population of the village, had gone away with their families to sea-side resorts, leaving neither friend nor foe worthy of William's mettle.

There were, however, two chief points of interest left. One was a group of new houses that was being built at the farther end of the village, and the other the field of Farmer Jenks's that was always let to campers in the summer. New houses meant new people, and William was always interested in new people. And Farmer Jenks's summer campers had afforded the Outlaws much entertainment in past years. There had been the League of Perfect Health—a miscellaneous assortment of weedy individuals who wore strange garments and indulged in strange antics and ran through the village with skipping-ropes or Indian clubs.

William hoped that the League of Perfect Health was coming again this year. Certainly, campers of some sort were coming, for a man had been round the field measuring out the ground, and a vanload of tents and equipment had been dumped in the middle. William divided his time between the field and the new houses. The houses, too, were ready for occupation, and families were beginning to arrive. They had so far proved disappointing, consisting solely of grown-ups of a particularly uninteresting brand. William, for want of anything better to do, hung over their gates and made conversational overtures to them, but was ignominiously repulsed on each occasion. Though two houses were still unoccupied, he had given up all hope of entertainment from that quarter and was now concentrating his whole attention upon the expected campers, when suddenly he saw two removing vans at the two unoccupied houses. Belongings were being taken out. He watched idly at first, then his eyes widened as he saw from one cricket bats, a hutch of rabbits and a football, and from the other a dolls' house and a scooter being unloaded. He didn't expect much from the dolls' house and scooter, of course, for girls were never any good, but he was at such a loose end that he couldn't help taking an interest even in the owner of a dolls' house and scooter. With regard to the owner of the cricket bat, rabbits and football he felt an overwhelming interest. Here, at any rate, was a boy, a contemporary, someone who, as friend or foe, would instil into life that spice of excitement that just now was so conspicuously lacking. He hung about till tea-time, but still the owners of the dolls' house and cricket bats had not arrived.

When he returned after tea, he found that they had arrived in his absence. He couldn't see the little girl, but he caught a glimpse of the boy through the window. He had red hair. He looked bigger and older than William, but not so much bigger and older as to be inaccessible. William's spirits rose. He'd come down first thing next morning and make friends with him. He'd show him all over the woods. He'd show him the owl's nest and the dead fox. He'd show him how to get into the empty house at the other end of the village. He'd show him the camping-field and tell him what fun the League of Perfect Health had been. If the League of Perfect Health came again he and the boy could bait them together. It wasn't any fun baiting people alone. . . .

He set off to the new houses directly after breakfast, and hung about in the road just outside. There was no sign of the boy with red hair, but after some minutes a little girl came round from the back of the other house, sucking a lollipop on a stick. She stood and looked at William over the gate.

"Hello," she said.

"Hello," said William.

"What's your name?"

"William. What's yours?"

"Lucinda."

William, with difficulty—for it was a friend he was looking for and not an enemy—refrained from adverse comment. She drew her lollipop out of her mouth and handed the stick to him. "You can finish it if you like," she said. "I've had enough. I had a whole box of them."

"Thanks awfully," said William gratefully.

He put the stick into his mouth, detached what was left of the lollipop, crunched it up, and swallowed it.

"You ought to have made it last longer than that," said Lucinda reproachfully.

"I don't like making things last," said William, and added: "What's your garden like at the back?"

"Same as this," said Lucinda, looking round at the trodden waste that formed the front garden. "We're going to have it done up properly when we've settled in."

"I like 'em like this," said William. "I don't know why people spoil 'em with grass an' flowers an' stuff. If I had a garden I'd have it all like this. You can't have any fun with flowers an' grass an' stuff."

"Would you like to come round an' see the back garden?" said Lucinda.

"Thanks," said William, and followed her round to the back of the house.

Here was a paradise of packing-cases, old tin cans, flotsam and jetsam of builder's materials, and the bare trodden earth that was William's ideal of a "garden."

"Gosh!" he ejaculated. "I wish ours was like this."

"You can play in it whenever you like," said Lucinda graciously.

Lucinda's graciousness was indeed a little over-powering. William wasn't used to graciousness in girls. They were generally aggressive and domineering, refusing to allow him to touch their things, and enlisting the aid of Authority against him on the slightest provocation.

William did not know, of course, that he had, as it were, caught Lucinda on the rebound, that Lucinda had that very morning made overtures of friendship to the red-haired boy and that her overtures had been curtly rejected. Lucinda wanted to *show* the red-haired boy, and the best way to do it seemed to be to enrol another boy in her service. She didn't really want William's admiration and friendship. She didn't want anyone's but the red-haired boy's. His rejection of her advances had raised him to a dizzy pinnacle in her estimation though she told herself that she hated and despised him. He had gone out that morning, and when he came back it was essential that he should see that she had a friend and admirer who was, in every way, his superior. Willlam didn't seem to be in any way his superior, but Lucinda was trying hard to imagine that he was. Anyway, he mustn't find her alone and neglected in the garden. He musn't think that she *still* wanted to be friends with him. He musn't think that she'd be friends with him now even if he *begged* her to be. (She had a pleasant mental picture of the red-haired boy's humbly begging her to come into his garden to play with him and of her turning away on her heel with her nose in the air. . . .)

William, of course, knew nothing of all this. He took her friendliness at its face value. He lorded it in her domain without let or hindrance. He made a boat out of the packing-cases. He found some cement, mixed it with water, and got it all over his face and hair. He climbed the only tree the garden offered and fell out of it on to his head. He picked himself up, arranged the packing-cases as stands for imaginary circus lions and put them through imaginary paces with much shouting and cracking of an imaginary whip, while Lucinda sat on an empty paint tin and formed the audience. Her meekness, her acquiescence in all his arrangements, went to his head, and he began to throw his weight about, boasting of his prowess in every field of valour.

"I'm not afraid of anyone," he shouted, swaggering about among the packing-cases and tin cans. "Not of anyone. An' I bet everyone's afraid of me. They've jolly well gotter be."

A gleam of interest came into Lucinda's eyes.

"Can you fight?" she said.

William laughed.

"Fight?" he said. "Me? I could be a prize-fighter if I wanted to be. I can fight people twice as big as me. Bash 'em all up so's——" he remembered the threat an irate lorry driver had used last winter when caught neatly by a snowball—"so's their own mothers won't know 'em."

"Do you often fight?" went on Lucinda eagerly.

"Often?" said William. "Me? I fight every day. Often two people. An' I jolly well beat 'em, too. All of 'em. Bash 'em all up."

"Would you fight someone for me?" said Lucinda cunningly.

"'Course I would," said William, "anyone you like."

"Will you fight a boy called Montague for me?" said Lucinda.

Though the red-haired boy had refused to speak to her, she had heard his mother call him Montague.

William was slightly taken aback by this abrupt transition from the realms of dream to the realms of reality.

"Well—er—why?" he countered. "What's he done?"

Lucinda found this hard to explain, so took refuge in an attitude of amazed indignation.

"So *that's* what you're like!" she said. "First you say you'll fight someone for me an' then you say you won't. I don't believe you *can* fight anyone."

"I can," persisted William. "Honest I can. I can fight anyone. I—I *will* fight him for you. Er—how big is he?"

"He'd be nothing to *you*," said Lucinda. "He's not twice as big as you, and, anyway, you said you could fight people twice as big as you."

"Yes, I can," said William hastily. "I can fight people twice as big as me all right. Three times as big as me. But—er—I don't know this boy Montague, so I don't see how I can fight him."

"I'll show you him," said Lucinda ruthlessly. "And he's not *much* bigger than you. Not *very* much."

"Oh . . ." said William, gazing blankly in front of him. "Oh . . . well, I can fight people all right, but—well, I'm very busy jus' now, so I don't know when I'll have the time to come round here again for you to show him to me. . . ."

Lucinda's eyes were bright with tears of anger.

"You said you would and now you won't and——"

"Yes, I will," said William, moved by the sight of the tears. "I promise I will."

"You'll do him same as you do the others?"

"Yes," agreed William.

"Bash him all up?"

"Yes," promised William.

"So his mother won't know him?"

"Er—yes," agreed William somewhat faintly. "How much bigger than me did you say he was?"

"Not very much bigger," said Lucinda. "Only a *few* years older, I should think. He's not twice as big, anyway, an' you said——"

"Yes, I know I did," said William rather irritably. "I know I did. Well, I will, too, soon as I know who he is, but I can't do anythin' without knowin' who he is."

"I've told you what he's like," said Lucinda. "He's a *horrid* boy. You can tell he's a horrid boy just by looking at him."

"All right," said William. "Well, I'd better be goin' back home now."

For suddenly the little back garden, so thrilling a playground a few moments ago, had lost its glamour. Even Lucinda looked less attractive, her hair less golden, her eyes less blue. It had been a jolly morning, but the whole affair was now at an end. He couldn't come here again and risk being introduced to the mysterious Montague, "not much bigger and only a few years older," whose annihilation he had so rashly undertaken.

Lucinda continued to be sweetly gracious to him as he took his departure, even running indoors to fetch him the rest of the box of lollipops. He thanked her in a preoccupied fashion, keeping an anxious eye on the horizon, prepared to bolt at the appearance of any large unknown boy. . . .

"You can come back and play with me this afternoon, too, if you like," called Lucinda, who had been much disappointed that Montague had not arrived in time to see the little charade that had been so carefully staged for his benefit and to receive fitting punishment at the hands of her new champion.

William walked briskly along the road homeward. It was the best back garden he'd ever played in, and it was a pity that he couldn't ever play there again, but he couldn't. It would be haunted for him in future by the spectre of the unknown Montague—a spectre that had already assumed colossal proportions in his imagination. William, when angered, could put up a fairly good fight even against odds, but to attack someone larger than himself on no provocation at all was quite another matter.

After lunch he went down to the field to see if the campers had yet arrived. Evidently they hadn't, but more equipment had come and already there was an air of activity about the place. Some men in shorts were putting up tents, and others were unpacking saucepans, tin cups and plates. So engrossed was William in watching these preparations through the hedge, that at first he did not notice that the red-haired boy of the new house was stationed at another convenient spot farther down the hedge, also watching. They turned and saw each other simultaneously. William approached the newcomer.

"Hello," he said.

"Hello," said the red-haired boy.

"What's your name?"

"Ralph. What's yours?"

William was conscious of a feeling of relief on hearing the name Ralph, for the red-haired boy was certainly bigger than William and looked pretty tough. He could not know, of course, that the red-haired boy's name was Ralph Montague, and that his name was a perennial source of contention between him and his mother, for his mother persisted in calling him Montague, while the red-haired boy, who disliked the name, always called himself Ralph. (His father compromised by calling him Ronty.)

"William. How old are you?"

It turned out that Ralph was thirteen, and, further, that his tastes and William's were identical. They spent the afternoon ranging the countryside together, William blissfully happy in the new friendship.

"I'M NOT AFRAID OF HIM," SAID WILLIAM.

"Come and see my rabbits," said Ralph finally. "They're prize ones."

William hesitated.

"There—there isn't any other boy but you in those new houses, is there?" he said carelessly.

"No," said Ralph. "Worse luck! They're all grown-up but one awful soppy kid. You'll come and see my rabbits, won't you?"

The temptation was irresistible. Probably the little girl wouldn't see him pass the house, and anyway, even

LUCINDA STAMPED HER FOOT. "WELL, FIGHT HIM, THEN.
YOU PROMISED YOU WOULD—COWARDY, COWARDY
CUSTARD!"

if she did, the mysterious Montague probably wouldn't
be there. Perhaps he was just someone she'd imagined.
Girls did silly things like that. His courage restored,
he accompanied Ralph down the lane. To his dismay
Lucinda stood at the gate. He was passing her with a
muttered shamefaced greeting (for it was clear that
Ralph was magnificently ignoring her existence), when
she suddenly cried out: "*There* he is! Why don't
you fight him?"

"Where?" said William, looking round.

"There!" she cried excitedly, pointing at Ralph.

"He's not called Montague," said William.

"He is. He *is*," said Lucinda, in a high-pitched squeak of excitement.

"You're not, are you?" said William to Ralph.

"Well, I am in a way," admitted Ralph, looking puzzled, "but I don't see——"

Lucinda stamped her foot, angry eyes fixed on William.

"You promised to fight him and now you won't. You said you weren't afraid of him and you are. You're a coward, that's what you are. You're afraid of him."

"I'm not afraid of him," said William with spirit.

"Well, go on. Fight him, then. You said you would. You're a coward and a story-teller."

"I'm not," said William.

"Well, fight him, then. You're afraid of him." She pointed a finger and began to jeer. "Cowardy cowardy custard!"

"I'm not afraid," said William hotly. He squared up to Ralph.

"Come on," he said.

"All right," said Ralph.

He didn't know what the fight was about, but one could always ask that afterwards.

William's fist shot out. Ralph parried it and got one in on William's eye that sent him rolling on to the ground. He got up and returned to the attack. Again his fist went wild and Ralph's got him neatly—this time on the nose—and felled him. After the third time Ralph said, "Want any more?" William gasped, "No thanks," and the two of them shook hands.

Then William turned a fast-closing eye apprehensively on to Lucinda. She was sobbing with rage and chargin.

"You said you'd b-b-bash him up," she sobbed, "an' it's you that's g-g-got b-b-bashed up. You're a horrid boy and a story-teller and I'll never speak to you again."

She turned and ran, still sobbing, into the house.

"What's it all about?" said the mystified Ralph.

"I don't know," said William. "She told me to fight you an' I said I would. I didn't know it was you."

"She's batty," said Ralph with careless conviction. "All girls are. Come on and see the rabbits."

As far as Ralph was concerned, that was the end of the incident. Girls didn't exist for him, and he continued to ignore Lucinda, thereby increasing daily the attraction he had for her and the hatred she bore him. William and he got on excellently. Together they ran wild over the countryside, ranged the woods and navigated (with only partial success) all the neighbouring ponds. Together they watched the arrival of the campers—the South London Boys' Guild, a band of young toughs who marched in procession, two and two, from the station, lustily singing camp songs.

After that it was their daily practice to go down to the field and watch the campers. Relations, of course, were soon established, relations which were—naturally, perhaps, in the circumstances—of a hostile character. William and Ralph jeered at the campers through the bars of the gates, pretending to offer them nuts and buns, and were pursued by furious bands of South London toughs, who, however, could not compete with them in fleetness of foot. They climbed a tree that overhung the camping-ground and hurled insults at the "cooks" who were preparing the midday meal just below. Isolated conflicts took place in which William and Ralph managed either to come off victors or escape altogether.

All William's boredom had vanished. He didn't even miss the Outlaws. Ralph's two-year seniority made his friendship a very flattering one, and he was as daring and regardless of consequences as William himself. But William couldn't quite forget Lucinda. He liked her. She'd been kind to him. He'd promised to bash Ralph all up for her, and he hadn't been able to. Quite obviously his name was now mud in Lucinda's eyes. When they met in the neighbourhood of Ralph's home she turned her head aside with an expression of supreme disgust, wrinkling up her small nose as though some rank smell had assailed it. Ralph did not notice this because Ralph did not notice her at all. To Ralph, Lucinda didn't exist. But the knowledge of Lucinda's scorn was a nagging discomfort at William's heart, a perpetual pinprick in his self-esteem. He'd enjoyed basking in the sunshine of her favour. The knowledge of her contempt was a very bitter one. Meantime, however, there was the countryside to be explored and hostilities against the South London toughs to be carried on with the exciting Ralph.

The last entertainment soon overreached itself, for a large man in spectacles and shorts had called on the parents of both Ralph and William to complain of the persistent annoyance that they were causing his campers. Both sets of parents were duly horrified and enraged.

"How any son of mine can behave so like a vulgar guttersnipe," said Mr. Brown, "is a mystery to me."

And Ralph's father said pretty much the same to

him, just as, thirty odd years ago, *their* fathers had said pretty much the same to them.

The two were finally forbidden even to approach the camping-field or to address any one of the campers.

"Remember, you are not to go into the lane that skirts the field on any excuse whatsoever, and you are never to speak to any of those boys again."

"Oh, well," said Ralph, meeting William next day, "there's plenty else to do."

But somehow the "plenty else" had lost its savour. They tried tracking each other through the woods and riding Farmer Jenks's prize pigs and getting on to the roof of the empty house, but there was no zest in these things.   The camping-field drew them as by a magnet.

"We can't go into the lane," said William, "but I bet we can see them all right from the field the other side of the lane.   That won't be *in* the lane."

They made their way to the field and tried to see through the two hedges, but it wasn't easy, and the glimpses of their foes were tantalisingly inadequate.

"There's Fatty carryin' that pail," said William. (They had endowed all their foes with opprobrious nicknames.)   "Must be his turn to help with breakfast. Who's with him?"

"Can't see," said Ralph.   "Let's get just a *bit* nearer. . . .   I say!   We needn't go *in* the lane exactly, but we could stand on the grass at the edge of it.   It's practically in the hedge and the hedge isn't the lane."

This reasoning appealed to William, and they scraped their way through the hedge to the lane and stood on the grass by the roadside, trying to watch the campers.

Maddeningly indistinct figures passed to and fro.

"Come on," said William.   "We might as well go

"THIS WAY TO WHIPSNADE," SHOUTED WILLIAM. "WATCH
THE MONKEYS TRYING TO PLAY CRICKET."

the other side of the lane. It'll be on the grass by the
hedge, same as this, and the grass isn't the lane, same
as you said. They only said we'd not to go *in* the lane."

"All right," said Ralph. "An' we can almost jump
over the lane so we won't have gone *in* it at all."

They jumped to the grass at the other side, and now
they were in their old position, with only a hedge
between them and the South Londoners.

"It's all right," said Ralph. "We won't say anything to them. We won't even let 'em know we're here,
an' that's just the same as not being here."

A BOY WHO HAD JUST DROPPED A CATCH CRIED, "LET'S GO
FOR THEM!"

This again was the sort of reasoning that appealed
to William.

" 'Course it is," he said. " They jus' meant that
we'd not got to call out at 'em. Well, we're not goin'
to, so it's all right.... Let's go along to the gate. We'll

see better there.   We'll keep behind the hedge, so they
won't see us, but we'll be able to see 'em better."

Having thus satisfied those hardy organs that did
duty as their consciences, they crept along behind the
hedge to the gate and, crouching down, watched under
cover of the hedge, whispering excitedly as the better
known of their foes appeared and disappeared among
the crowd of boys near the gate.

"There's ole Fatty again. . . . Look! There's ole
Scarecrow. He's getting up a game of cricket. . . .
There's Goggle. . . . What's he doin'? . . . Oh, I
say! Look, there's ole Bandy Legs. . . . Got his
arm in a sling. . . . 'Spect a ball hit his bat by
mistake when he was playin' cricket, an' it gave him
such a shock it sprained his arm. . . . There's ole Flat-
face. . . . He's limping. . . . Must have sprained his
ankle running away from a moth. . . . He's scared
stiff of moths. . . . There's ole Nosey. . . . Looks
sick, don't he? . . . 'Spect he couldn't manage to
pinch someone else's breakfast as well as his own to-
day. . . . Look at ole Beefy. . . ."

Gradually the two had come out of the cover of the
hedge and were standing on the bottom rung of the
gate, leaning over the top. Gradually the comments,
from being furtive whispers, became insults hurled at
the tops of their voices.

"This way to Whipsnade," shouted William.

"Penny each to feed the monkeys," shouted Ralph.

"Watch the monkeys tryin' to play cricket."

The cricket game was in progress just near the gate,
and each failure of fielder or batsman was greeted with
derisive cheers and ironical comments by William and
Ralph.

Suddenly, as at a preconcerted signal, the players left the game and rushed towards the gate. A young stalwart thrust his fist into William's face, but overbalanced with the effort and fell down. William turned to flee, followed by Ralph, and did not stop till he had put several fields between himself and the camping-ground. Then he realised that Ralph was no longer with him. There was in fact no sign of him. Cautiously he retraced his steps.

It wasn't till he'd almost reached the camping-ground that he met him, and stood gazing at him in silent horror. His nose was bleeding, his lip was cut, both eyes were rapidly blackening and closing. There was a large bruise on his forehead and he limped painfully as he walked.

"Gosh!" gasped William at last.

"Yes," agreed Ralph bitterly. "The whole lot of 'em set on me and I hadn't a chance. An' it's nothin' to what my father'll do to me when he finds I've been there again."

This aspect of the affair struck William for the first time.

"You've got a jolly black eye yourself," went on Ralph with a certain satisfaction. "I bet you'll get in as big a row as me."

"We needn't say they did it," said William. "They won't say anythin' about it 'cause they aren't supposed to fight. It's one of their rules."

"But what can we say?"

"Let's say we got tossed by a bull."

"No, we can't. Farmer Jenks's bull's locked up an' there aren't any more round here."

"Let's say a train ran into us."

"No, these don't look like train marks. Besides,

that would be just as bad, 'cause we've been told not to go on the embankment."

"Tell you what!"

"What?"

"Let's say we fought each other."

Ralph considered the suggestion without enthusiasm.

"But you've only got a black eye," he objected, "and I'm in an awful mess. I bet if we'd fought each other I'd have had nothing at all and you'd have been all messed up."

"Yes," agreed William, "but it's better than gettin' in a row for goin' *there* again."

"It is for you," said Ralph morosely. It was humiliating enough to have been so completely beaten even against overwhelming odds, but to have to attribute his injuries to a boy several inches shorter and two years his junior——"Very well," he said at last, reluctantly. "It's better than getting in another row, I s'pose. I wouldn't go near their beastly field again, not if they paid me to, would you?"

"No," said William; "anyway, they aren't likely to."

William's spirits were rising. For a glorious possibility had suddenly occurred to him. At last he could win back Lucinda's good graces, the loss of which had caused him so much secret chagrin. At last he would seem to have done her bidding. Ostensibly he and Ralph had engaged in mortal combat, and there was no doubt at all who had come off victor. He saw Lucinda again smiling at him sweetly, gazing up at him admiringly. He'd go and play in her back garden again on the afternoons when Ralph went out with his mother, as he sometimes had to. . . .

He accompanied Ralph home. To his intense

gratification Lucinda was standing at her front window. She watched them, open-mouthed with interest and amazement. Certainly neither of them was a sightly object, but Ralph was horrible. William put on the swagger of the victor as he passed the window.

He took his leave of Ralph at his gate.

"You'd better not come in," said Ralph. "They'll only make a worse fuss if they see you, too."

Ralph walked up the garden path, turned at the door to wave farewell, and disappeared.

Lucinda was already hastening down the garden path. William approached her with a swagger.

"Well, you told me to, didn't you?" he said. "I didn't know why you wanted me to, but when I say I'll do a thing I jolly well do it . . ."

"Did you do *that* to him?" gasped Lucinda.

William shrugged with the air of one who modestly accepts a merited distinction.

"An' anyone else you want all bashed up you've only gotter ask me," he said. "I wasn't tryin' that time you saw me. I wanted to do it prop'ly sometime when you weren't there. He's bigger'n me, but I never think of that when I want to bash someone all up. I——"

He realised at this point that there was something strange in Lucinda's expression. It was not the complacent expression of one whose champion has just avenged her on her enemy. The light in her eye was not one of admiration. He tried to dodge but it was too late.

"You horrid boy!" she screamed. "You beastly bully! You wicked, cruel boy! I hate you—I *hate* you. I'll never forgive you as long as I live. . . ."

Biting, scratching, tugging at his hair, she drove him down the road. . . .

B

CHAPTER II

WHAT'S IN A NAME?

THE idea of a Boy Sanctuary, which had occurred to William on the day when he had set out on his (never completed) tour of the world, continued to simmer idly at the back of his mind. It was the sight of a Bird Sanctuary, complete with coconuts, nuts, pieces of cake, bird tables, and bird baths, that had suggested the idea. Why should birds be thus petted and pampered, he had thought, and boys neglected? It wasn't fair. . . . His mind's eye saw a pleasant strip of woodland, with sweets and cakes and biscuits neatly ranged on "boy tables", doughnuts hanging from the trees, cream buns concealed among the moss, "boy baths" full of lemonade or ginger pop. . . . It was an attractive picture, and he couldn't think why it had never occurred to any of the grim-faced old ladies who took such care to lay out crumbs and nuts for birds, to lay out a few dainties for passing boys, on the same principle. He even suggested it to one or two of them, but the suggestion was so coldly received that he did not repeat it.

"Birds!" he said to himself indignantly. "Can't do enough for *birds*, but *boys* can starve, for all they care! Birds what haven't anythin' to do but play about an' enjoy themselves all day long, singin' an' such like, an' we've gotter go to school an' work till we're wore out, an' no one ever gives us anythin'."

One old lady even took in a magazine about them, called *Our Feathered Friends*. William had had serious thoughts of starting a rival called *Our Suited Friends*, dealing entirely with boys and their interests, but had judged from the general attitude that it would not have a large circulation, and had reluctantly dropped the idea. Still, though he realised that there was little hope of his Boy Sanctuary's being taken up as a philanthropic scheme, he was loth to abandon it altogether. It might have possibilities as a commercial proposition. A small piece of one of the neighbouring woods hung with dainties . . . a penny admission charged. . . . But the idea bristled with difficulties. Clients would be sure to enter without paying their penny, or, if they did pay their penny, to eat more than their pennyworth.

It was while he was wandering over the countryside, cogitating this problem, that he came upon the empty house and garden down the lane off the Jenks's farm. It was called Gorse View, and seemed to have been empty for some time, for the To Be Sold notice was faded and weather-beaten. There were no neighbours to object to his going into the garden, so he went into it and spent a very pleasant afternoon there. It was not a large garden, but it was what William considered a very sensible one. It consisted of a lawn in front of the house, with a thick spinney running down one side of it. A small gate led into the spinney from the lane, and an overgrown path wound through it among tall trees and rampant brambles. An ideal place for the Boy Sanctuary. . . . The gate would regulate the stream of clients and ensure the payment of the entrance fee; the dainties could be half concealed among the moss and brambles and hung from the branches of the trees. Some trees had been cut down, and their stumps would afford convenient "boy tables". There was even a battered bird bath on the lawn, which William lugged into the spinney and set by the side of the path. That, of course, would be filled with lemonade, and the penny entrance fee would include two laps each. But still the difficulties were enormous. How was he to prevent the clients from eating each more than his due share, and, most difficult of all, how was he to provide the necessary capital for floating the scheme? Though in imagination William saw the woodland path set out with buns and sweets and cakes, and a neat procession of clients entering the little gate and duly paying their pennies to William as they entered, the vision had that hazy unreality that belongs to visions difficult, if not impossible, of attainment. However, William thought it quite worth discussing with his Outlaws, and he would have discussed it that very evening if everything else had not been driven out of their minds by the sight of a man in a black shirt standing on a wooden box in the middle of the village, just outside the Blue Lion, shouting hoarsely at a small and somewhat bewildered audience. The Outlaws promptly joined the audience. They couldn't make out much of what the speaker was saying, but he looked very noble and magnificent, perched up aloft on his wooden box, in his black shirt, shouting and throwing his arms about. It made William and the Outlaws long to be up there, too, shouting and throwing their arms about. Then two other men in black shirts joined him, and they all saluted each other in a fiercely military fashion, after which they distributed leaflets, marched to a small sports car that was waiting for them, and drove off at

a dizzy speed. William and the Outlaws watched
wistfully. The salutes, the shouting, the final departure in the very noisy sports car, had all been most
impressive. They made ordinary life seem dull and
uneventful. They even made William's Boy Sanctuary
seem childish and absurd. No, he wouldn't waste his
time over things like Boy Sanctuaries. He'd stand on a
box and shout and wave his arms about and salute
people.

"Who were they?" he said with interest.

"Black shirts," said Henry, who always seemed to
know everything. "They're fascists."

"What do they want?"

"They want to be dictators and make everyone do
what they want 'em to. An' then there's Brown shirts
an'—an' Red 'uns. They're called Communists, the
red 'uns."

"What do *they* want?" asked William.

"Oh, they jus' want to be the dictators, same as the
others, an' make everyone do what they want 'em to.
An' they all shout'n' salute'n' that sort of thing."

"It sounds jolly," said William. "Do children do
it, too?"

"Yes," said Henry. "I saw 'em at the pictures
once. All in black shirts. Drillin' an' such like."

"Well, we could, then," said William, brightening.

"We've not got any black shirts," objected Douglas.

"We can black 'em with ink," suggested Ginger.

"No, we can't," said William. "You know what
a fuss they make when ink gets on 'em natural. They'd
make an *awful* fuss if we blackened 'em prop'ly."

"What can we do, then?" said Ginger.

"Well, we needn't have black shirts," said William.

"We'd rather not, come to that, 'cause they'd only think we'd been copyin' them, an' we don't want 'em to think we've been copyin' them. We won't have black *or* brown *or* red. We'll have a different colour altogether."

"Well, how're we goin' to get 'em?" demanded Douglas, who had an irritating habit of being practical. "We've only got white shirts, anyway, an' no one's likely to buy us any others, an' we've not got any money ourselves, so——"

He left the sentence unfinished. They looked at him a little reproachfully. They'd all been seeing themselves as magnificent figures in coloured shirts, saluting and shouting and throwing their arms about, and it was unpleasant to be brought down to earth so abruptly.

"Let's ask for them for our Christmas presents— I mean, say we'll have 'em now to do for our Christmas presents. I bet they'll have forgotten when Christmas comes an' give us somethin' else as well."

"No," said William gloomily. "I've often tried that for things. They won't do it. They're too mean."

"Well, how do these other people get theirs?"

"I 'spect the government gives them them."

"Well, why shu'n't they give them us?"

"They won't," said Henry with conviction. "They never give anyone anythin', the government don't. You should hear the way my father goes on about them."

"I say," said William, struck by a sudden idea, "We could wear our ordin'ry shirts an' a coloured band round the arm. I've seen people doin' that in pictures."

"That's a jolly fine idea," said Ginger approvingly. "What colour'll we have?"

"We'll jolly well have to wait till we see what we can get," said William cautiously. "T'isn't as if we'd got any money. I'll have to see if I can pinch anythin' from Ethel. She gets stuff like that for hats an' things."

"Yes, an' as soon as we start it that ole Hubert Lane an' his gang'll copy it," said Ginger. "Same as they did our Mayor an' Corp'ration. They can never think of anythin' themselves."

"Well, let 'em," said William. "It'll make it more excitin'. They'll do for the enemy."

"What'll we call ourselves?"

"It'll depend what colour we can get. We'll all have a good try to get a colour to-night."

They all had a good try and assembled with their spoils the next morning. Ginger had found an old tie of his father's in the rag-bag. Douglas had taken some purple ribbon trimming from an old hat of his mother's that was among the Rummage Stall contributions on the spare-room bed. Henry had surreptitiously removed the ribbon bow from the neck of his small sister's Teddy Bear.

"An' she'll make an awful fuss when she finds out," he said apprehensively. "I never knew anyone like her for makin' a fuss about nothin'."

William, however, had struck lucky. Ethel had run out of stamps and had asked him to go into the village to get some for her. William, as usual, had demanded compensation for his trouble. He had demanded it with unusual politeness, even meekness. "I don' want money, Ethel," he had said, "but if you've got jus' a bit of ole ribbon you can let me have I'd be jolly grateful."

Ethel was touched by the unusual humility of his

manner. Moreover, she had no halfpennies in her purse and certainly did not mean to give William more than a halfpenny. It happened, too, that she had been tidying her drawers that afternoon and had found a length of peculiarly virulent green ribbon, which she had once been misguided enough to buy at a sale. She had dropped it into her waste-paper basket with a shudder, but her mind now turned to it as a possible solution of the problem.

"What do you want ribbon for?" she said suspiciously.

"Well, I—er—sort of want it," said William mysteriously. "It's a secret why I want it. A jolly important secret. You'll be jolly grateful to me one day. It's somethin' to do with the gov'nment."

"Rubbish!" said Ethel. "Anyway, if you really want some ribbon, I've got a beautiful piece upstairs that I'll give you. But——" for Ethel was more commercial minded than her ethereal looks would have led one to suppose—"it'll have to do for more than just going once to the post-office. You'll have to do three things for that."

"What three things?" said William, suspicious in his turn.

"Well, I don't know yet," said Ethel. "Into the village or upstairs or anything I want you to do. It's beautiful ribbon."

"I'll do two for you for it," offered William.

"Three."

"Two."

"Three."

"Two."

"Three."

"IT'S A SECRET WHY I WANT IT," SAID WILLIAM MYSTERI-
OUSLY. "IT'S SOMETHIN' TO DO WITH SAVIN' THE COUNTRY."

"Well, let me see it."

"It's upstairs. You can fetch it. I—er—put it in
my waste-paper basket, because I thought it was a
nice safe place for it. It's beautiful ribbon. I don't
really want to give it away."

"Well, can going up for it count for one?"

"Very well," agreed Ethel, who was getting tired of the argument. "It can count for one. Then you'll have to do another, besides going for the stamps, if I give you the ribbon."

"All right," said William, "but it's not to be anywhere but upstairs or jus' to the village. I'm not fielding tennis balls for it or anythin' like that."

"You're not exactly going to put yourself out, are you?" said Ethel sarcastically.

William was already half-way upstairs, so made no retort to this. He returned a few moments later with the ribbon.

"Yes, it's jolly nice," he said. "Thanks awfully. I'll field tennis balls once for it, if you like."

"I don't suppose we'll want you to," said Ethel generously. "You're not much good at it, anyway. You generally start doing something on your own and forget all about it. Anyway, you can go and get me those stamps now."

William put the ribbon in his pocket, fetched the stamps, then set off to join his Outlaws at the old barn. The ribbon, about two inches wide, was enough to make armlets for them all. Henry promised to get the necessary safety-pins to-morrow from his little sister's nursery.

"We'll call ourselves the Green shirts," said William, "an' we'll do same as the others—drill an' salute an' make speeches an' all that."

Henry brought the safety-pins the next morning (he had been pursued down the road by the nurse, who had, unfortunately, seen him take them), and Ginger hacked the ribbon into four pieces with a very blunt penknife, then, discarding their coats, they slipped the armlets up their sleeves and at once began to drill energetically under William's leadership. After that they marched in military fashion through the village, then William stood on a stile by the roadside and harangued them, throwing out his arms, in the fashion of his model as he emphasised his points.

"You've gotter have a dictator . . . you've all gotter be Green shirts same as us. . . . We're goin' to fight everyone that isn't. . . . We're goin' to fight everyone in the world. . . . We're goin' to conquer the world. . . . We're goin' to be dictators over the world."

He then saluted Henry, Ginger, and Douglas, and they all marched on through the village.

As Ginger had foretold, this proceeding attracted the attention of the Hubert Laneites. Hubert Lane himself approached them as they marched past his house, looking cautious and inquisitive, followed by Bertie Franks.

"What're *you* doing?" said Hubert, trying to speak carelessly, but obviously consumed by curiosity.

"Never you mind," said William, not because he didn't mean to tell Hubert, but in order to whet his curiosity the further.

"Go on—tell us," said Hubert, a nauseating note of coaxing in his voice.

"You'll know soon enough," said William, in a tone that he strove to make menacing and sinister. "You'll know all right when you wake up one morning an' find yourself in a dungeon an' us dictators."

Hubert Lane looked slightly taken aback. Then he rallied his forces.

"Go on!" he said. "Who'd make you dictators?"

"We'll make ourselves," said William darkly. "It'll all happen quite sudden. They're gettin' the dungeons ready for you now."

Hubert Lane went slightly pale, but Bertie Franks rallied to his chief's rescue.

"Dungeon yourself!" he said. "Anyway, what *are* you?"

"Green shirts," said William. "An' we're goin' to be dictators over the whole world."

"Can anyone join?" said Hubert anxiously.

"No," said William. "We don't want *you*, anyway. We're very partic'lar who we have in the Green shirts. We're goin' to have *you* in the dungeon."

He started forward, winking at his followers, and added: "Come on! Let's capture him now."

Hubert and Bertie ran off as fast as their fat legs could carry them. The Outlaws pretended to pursue them for a few yards, then returned to the old barn, where William drilled them again and made a few more speeches.

The next day Hubert and his followers appeared in white shirts with handsome broad blue ribbons round their arms.

"We're the Blue shirts," shouted Hubert from the safe refuge of his garden hedge, "an' we're jolly well goin' to get a dungeon for *you*."

"Oh, you are, are you?" retorted William. "Well how're you goin' to manage it, shut up in one yourself?"

Exchanging similar pleasantries, the two bands patrolled the village, drilling and marching and making speeches. Hubert couldn't think of anything to say himself, so he simply repeated what he heard William say. He also avoided meeting the Green shirts, contenting himself with hurling insults at them over the hedge, as they marched past his garden.

"Come out and have a fight!" William would shout. "We're ready for you."

But the Hubert Laneites would never come out and have a fight.

There didn't, therefore, seem very much to do except march about and drill, salute each other, and make speeches of a very limited scope, and the Outlaws would soon have tired of the affair had not the Hubert Laneites introduced a new element into it.

"Yah!" called Hubert Lane to them over the hedge one morning as they marched past. "We've gotter col'ny."

William stopped.

"A what?" he said.

"A col'ny," said Hubert. He climbed up on to a garden seat and grinned down at them. He looked very fat and smug in his white shirt with the broad blue armlet. Through the hedge the Outlaws could see the other Blue shirts standing in a group, listening. "Don't you know what a col'ny is?"

"*Course* I do," said William hastily. "I know a jolly sight more about col'nies than what you do."

"Well, all these shirt people want col'nies," said Hubert. "I heard my father talkin' about it yest'day an' my aunt's given us her garden for a col'ny so we've gotter col'ny an' you haven't. *Yah!*"

"Oh, you think we've not gotter col'ny, do you?" said William, with what was meant to be a short, dry laugh. "Oh, that's what you think, is it? Well, you'd be jolly surprised if you knew about *our* col'ny.

It's a jolly sight better than any ole aunt's garden, I can tell you."

"Where is it, then?" said Hubert, incredulous but impressed, despite himself, by William's manner.

"You'd like to know, wouldn't you?" said William, repeating the short, dry laugh not very successfully, and quickly moving his followers on beyond earshot.

"What *is* a col'ny?" he said, as soon as they had safely turned the bend in the road.

"It's a place where c'lonials live," said Douglas. "My cousin knows some c'lonials. They're jus' the same as English, but they talk a bit different."

"Why should these shirt people want 'em?"

Even Henry was rather vague on this point.

"I dunno," he said, "but I bet I can find out."

When they next met they gathered from the somewhat complacent expression on Henry's face that he had managed to find out, to his own satisfaction at any rate.

"They want col'nies," he said, "cause there's food and stuff there."

"I bet you're thinking of a sankcherry," said William.

"A what?"

"A sankcherry. Bird sankcherry an' boy sankcherry an' such like. Nuts an' stuff everywhere."

"Dunno about that," said Henry vaguely, "but it's col'nies these shirt people want."

"An' *they've* got one," Ginger reminded them.

"I bet they haven't really," said William. "They were jus' swankin'. I *bet* they've not got one. I bet no one's aunt would give 'em a garden. Not if they're anythin' like *my* aunts, anyway. Where does his aunt live? Let's go'n see."

A few cautious enquiries led to the discovery of Hubert's aunt's address, and the Green shirts set off at a march to investigate matters further.

"Messin' it all up with col'nies and stuff!"grumbled Ginger. "They never can leave anythin' alone. Green shirts an' Blue shirts were all right, but—*col'nies!*"

Hubert's aunt lived at a cottage at the other end of the village. She was one of the more foolish kind of aunts and shared with Hubert's mother the delusion that Hubert was sweet. She thought everything he said and did wonderful and she gave him pennies whenever she met him. And there, sure enough, was a large notice on the gate—"Blue Shirts Col'ny"—with a small blue flag waving above.

The Green shirts looked cautiously about, but there was no sign of the Blue shirts.

"Let's get away quick before they see us an' start swankin," said William.

They marched on quickly down the road.

"We'll have to get one now," said Ginger firmly.

"Y-yes," agreed William.

His imagination had visualised his "Boy Sanctuary" at Gorse View, set out with nuts and sweets and cakes, so plainly that he could hardly believe that it wasn't actually there, stocked with dainties, his own private property. It would make a wonderful col'ny. . . . It would knock Hubert's aunt's garden hollow.

"Yes," Henry was saying, "we'll have to get something. Let's all think over our aunts."

They all thought over their aunts. It was a depressing meditation. Their faces grew longer and blanker.

"Mine won't even let me go into her garden," said Douglas, bitterly, "much less give it me."

All the Outlaws seemed similarly situated with regard to aunts and aunts' gardens.

"I never *meant* to fall through her old greenhouse," said Ginger. "I was only jus' trying to climb over it, an' ever since then she's not even let me go inside her gate."

It appeared that Henry, having been asked recently by his aunt to post a letter, had forgotten all about it, and it had stayed in his pocket for a week. It had been, according to Henry's aunt, a most important letter. ("Askin' ole Mrs. Monks to tea!" said Henry, in disgust. "As if *that* was important!") and they were now not on speaking terms, while William, after an unsuccessful attempt to graft one of her new apple trees on to another, according to some instructions that he had read in the paper, had been forbidden by his aunt ever to enter her garden again.

"We do have rotten luck in aunts," said William, wistfully. "The only ones I have that are nice to me an' give me things are the ones I never see. Seems sort of queer."

By a strange coincidence the others were in the same plight. The only aunts they had who were really nice to them were the ones they never saw. . . .

"An' a fat lot of use *they* are when you want a col'ny," went on William, bitterly.

Their own gardens were, of course, out of the question. They were all on strained relations with their respective gardeners, and their every movement there was regarded with jealous suspicion. The problem seemed for the moment to be insoluble.

"Anyway, theirs isn't much of a col'ny," said William. "There's no food or anythin' in it." Again his thoughts turned to the colony-sanctuary of his dreams—the fascinating spinney of Gorse View and all the dainties with which his imagination had so freely provided it. "It's jolly well nothin' to one I could show 'em."

"Well, let's go back an' see what they're doin'," suggested Ginger.

They went down the road in military fashion, led by William, till they reached Hubert's aunt's garden again.

The Blue shirts were now there, marching about the garden, not very briskly, shouting: "We've gotter col'ny, a col'ny, a col'ny. We've gotter col'ny an' the rotten ole Green shirts haven't."

The Outlaws were going to tip-toe past, so as not to give the Hubert Laneites the satisfaction of knowing that they had heard their gibe, when the face of Hubert Lane appeared suddenly over the hedge. It lit up with malicious triumph on seeing the Green shirts, and he pointed exultantly to the flag and notice on the gate.

"Who's gotter col'ny an' who's not?" he said.

The other Blue shirts took up the refrain.

"Who's gotter col'ny? Who's gotter col'ny?"

William stared at him coldly.

"Call *that* a col'ny?" he said, with a contemptuous sweep of his hand. "Gosh! You should see ours."

So convincing was his manner that Hubert was disconcerted.

"What's wrong with it?" he demanded, indignantly. "It's a jolly good col'ny."

"Oh, is it?" said William. "Well, it's not got any food in it, for one thing. That's what they have col'nies for—to get food from 'em. Thought everyone knew that."

"Well, you've not got one at all," countered Hubert, "so you needn't talk."

"Oh, haven't we?" said William. "Let *me* tell *you* we have, an' a jolly sight better than this one."

In his mind's eye Gorse View was becoming clearer and clearer, hung with doughnuts, festooned with cream buns. . . .

"Where is it, then?" challenged Hubert.

"Yes, where is it? chorused the other Blue shirts.

William hesitated, and they seized triumphantly upon his hesitation.

"You've not got one! You've not got one! *Yah!* You've not got one."

"We have."

"You haven't."

"We have."

"You haven't."

"We have."

"All right. Where is it, then?" said Hubert again. And the Blue shirts, as usual, took up the refrain.

"Yah, where is it? *Yah!* Where is it?"

"I'll tell you where it is," said William, throwing discretion to the winds. "It's called Gorse View, an' it's down the lane off Jenks's farm, an' it's full of stuff to eat, an' it licks your silly old aunt's garden hollow."

They stared at him, as convinced for the moment as was William himself of the truth of his statement.

"All right," said Hubert, quickly recovering his aplomb. "Take us there and show us it."

"Huh!" said William, with his short, dry laugh. "Think we're goin' to take *you* to our col'ny? Think we've no more sense that *that?*"

"Yah!" they cried, delightedly. "You've not got one. You've not got a col'ny. We knew you'd not got one all the time. *Yah!*"

"All right," said William. "You come an' see it. Come and see it to-night at six o'clock."

He had a vague idea that a few hours' respite would enable him to do something in the matter—he wasn't sure what.

"You'll not set on us if we do?" said Hubert, suddenly anxious.

"No. Not if you come at six. If you come before, we jolly well will," said William.

Hubert's small, shifty eyes moved to the other Green shirts—Ginger, Douglas and Henry—noting the blank expression on their faces. They hadn't got a colony. He was sure of it. A cunning look came into his eyes.

"Did you say there was food in it?" he said.

"Yes," said William, "lots of it. All sorts of food. Doughnuts and cream buns. That sort of food."

"Well, if it's not jus' same as you say, will you s'render to us an' give up bein' Green shirts?"

William hesitated. He hadn't been prepared for this.

"If it *is* same as you say," went on Hubert, suavely, "we'll s'render to you an' give up being Blue shirts."

He winked at his followers. He was now fully convinced that the Outlaws were bluffing and did not possess a colony of any kind, much less one of the kind described by William.

William looked at his enemy, saw the malicious grins on their faces, and committed himself finally.

"All right," he said, "if it *is* same as I said, you'll s'render to us, an' if it isn't we'll s'render to you."

" An' you'll be there at six?" said Hubert, anxiously.

"Yes," said William, then, afraid of entangling himself yet more deeply, though this would have been hardly possible, turned to the others with: "Come on! Quick march!"

The Green shirts set off down the road, pursued by derisive cat-calls from the Blue shirts' colony.

"Now!" said Ginger. "Look what you've let us in for! " What're we goin' to do *now?*"

"Well, it is a real place—this Gorse View," said William, somewhat feebly. "It's as good as their place, anyway."

"Yes, but look at all what you said about food in it," went on Ginger, reproachfully. "What're we goin' to do about that?"

"Well, I was sort of thinkin' it with food in it," explained William, a note of apology in his voice. "I'd forgot for the moment it hadn't any, really."

"Well, what're we goin' to *do?*"

"We could put some food in."

"Not the sort you said. We've not got any money, an' the sort of food we could pinch off the cook or get out of the dustbin wouldn't be the sort you said. It wouldn't count."

"An' six o'clock, too. That's only jus' after tea. It doesn't give us time to do anything. If you'd said to-morrow even, we might rescue someone from death an' get a reward, or someone might die an' leave us a lot of money, but six o'clock doesn't leave time for anythin'."

"Let's jus' not turn up at six," suggested Henry. "Let's pretend we were having him on."

"No, we can't do that," said William. "We promised."

"Let's pretend to-day's same as the first of April."

"No, we can't do that, either," said William. "Not when we've promised."

"It'll be jolly nice havin' to s'render to them," said Douglas, bitterly.

"Well, anyway," said William, "let's go'n' have a look at the place. S'no use jus' standin' here an' talkin' about it."

The gloomy attitude of the others was rousing all his native optimism. Anything might happen before six. . . .

"Come on," he said again, cheerfully. "Quick march!"

They marched along the road and down the lane to Gorse View. And there William stopped, dismayed to see, over the battered, almost indecipherable To Be Sold notice, a brand new, glaringly red strip, SOLD. No longer, then, was it a legitimate playground—an empty, ownerless house. It now had mysterious Occupiers, who might swoop down at any moment. They had evidently been there quite recently. There were deck-chairs on the lawn that had not been there before, and a large packing-case on the verandah. William reconnoitred cautiously round the house and garden. The new owners were certainly not on the premises now. His spirits rose. Perhaps they'd stay away till after six, at any rate. His spirits fell again. The problem of the food was still unsolved. He returned to the Green shirts at the gate.

"S'all right," he said. "There's no one here."

They came in and wandered about the spinney.

"You see, it makes a jolly good col'ny," said William, proudly.

"Yes, it'd be all right if you'd not promised 'em food," agreed Ginger.

"Well, anyway," said William, "let's go home an' see if we can find any food."

"We're likely to, aren't we?" said Ginger, sarcastically. "They'll say 'Wait till tea-time', if we say we're hungry, an' you can't get anythin' out of the larder without them seein' an' makin' a fuss."

"Well, we can have a try, can't we?" William rallied him. "You can have a try at anythin'. It doesn't do any harm. S'better than jus' talkin' about it!"

They walked down the lane to the main road. A motor was passing at a terrific speed. A basket hamper was fastened on to the back, and as the car passed the Outlaws the hamper fell to the ground. The Outlaws shouted, to draw the driver's attention. He turned in his seat, making the car swerve dangerously, glared angrily from them to the basket lying in the middle of the road, shook his fist at them, then disappeared round the bend at a breakneck speed.

The Outlaws stared at each other, then at the hamper.

"He *saw* it all right," said Ginger.

"P'raps it's empty."

"P'raps it's somethin' he doesn't want."

"P'raps it's bombs. He looked that sort of man."

"P'raps it's got someone he's murdered in it."

They approached the hamper cautiously, and stood round it. William bent his ear to it.

"Can't hear anythin' movin' or breathin'," he said. "I don't think it's anythin' alive."

"I bet it's someone he's murdered," said Ginger. "He was gettin' rid of the body, same as they do in

WILLIAM LIFTED THE LID, THEN STOPPED STILL, PARALYSED
BY AMAZEMENT.

books an' the newspaper. That's why he was so mad
when we shouted out to him."

"P'raps we'd better go away," suggested Douglas,
nervously.

"Let's jus' look inside, anyway," said William.
"Then if it *is* a body we can go an' tell the police."

"They'll say we did it," Douglas warned him.
"We'll prob'ly all get put in prison."

"Well, it'll be a change, anyway," said William. "I've often wanted to try what it's like bein' in prison."

He began to undo the straps that fastened the lid. The others watched a little apprehensively.

"P'raps it's bombs," said Douglas, "wound up to go off as soon as the lid's opened."

"*Bet* it's a body," persisted Ginger.

Slowly William lifted up the lid, then stood paralysed by amazement. Buns, doughnuts, cream cakes, biscuits, bottles of lemonade, large glistening iced cakes, sandwiches, sausage rolls, apples, bananas, sweets. . . .

It was a feast such as a starving man might have pictured in his delirium. The Outlaws stared at it in silence, their eyes growing wider and wider.

"Gosh!" said William at last, in a faint voice.

"Fancy him not stoppin' to pick up *that!*" said Ginger.

Douglas laid a tentative finger on the nearest sausage roll.

"It's real," he gasped.

"We ought to tell the p'lice," said Henry.

"We jolly oughtn't," retorted William, indignantly. "If it'd been a body we'd've told 'em all right, but we're jolly well not goin' to tell 'em about this. They've no more right to it than what we have. Why should *they* eat it 'stead of us? They're all a jolly sight too fat already. 'Sides, 'tisn't as if the man what was drivin' the car didn't know he'd dropped it. He turned right round and saw it. He—I *say!*" His eyes opened wide as this aspect of the affair struck him suddenly. "It'll do for the col'ny. It'll make it a *jolly* fine col'ny. Come on! Let's carry it there quick."

They staggered down the lane with the heavy basket
and took it in at the narrow gate of the spinney. The
red SOLD notice caused William a moment's uneasiness, but only a moment's.

"Bet they won't come to-day, even if they have
bought it," he reassured himself. "If they'd been
comin' to-day they'd've come by now, an' anyway
we'll be out of it soon after six. Come on. Let's
get the stuff out quick."

They worked hard at the pleasant task, putting the
sandwiches, sausage rolls, cream buns, and doughnuts
here and there along the side of the path, on the stumps
of the cut-down trees, in the bushes, and (Ginger ran
home for some string) hanging them from the lowest
branches of the trees. Then they emptied the bottles
of lemonade into the bird bath that William had
moved from the lawn.

Occasionally they paused for refreshment, but so
busy were they, and so lavish were the refreshments
that their inroads made little or no difference to them.
When they had finished, William gazed at the scene
with the deep satisfaction of the artist whose vision is
accomplished, whose ideal is realised. His Boy
Sanctuary. His Colony. What did the name matter?
Thus he had seen it in imagination weeks ago, and thus
it was now in very fact.

It was while he was standing, wrapped in a haze of
self-satisfaction, that he heard voices at the big front
gate that opened from the lawn on to the lane. He
peeped cautiously out of the spinney. A woman was
getting out of a taxi at the gate. She was short and
plump and looked very hot and worried, and she was
relating some lengthy adventure to the taxi-driver.

"Well, if I see any sign of it, 'm," he said, when she had finished, "I'll let you know at once."

She paid him and turned into the garden.

William had been too much interested in the scene to withdraw into the spinney when she turned, and her eyes fell on him as soon as she began to make her way towards the house.

"Come here, boy," she said.

To William's surprise she seemed rather relieved than annoyed to see him.

He advanced towards her cautiously.

"Move the deck-chairs into the shade first of all," said the lady.

Mystified, William moved the deck-chairs into the shade, then awaited developments.

"Do you live near here, boy?" went on the lady, as she sank down into the chair and began to mop her brow.

"Yes, I kind of do," admitted William, guardedly.

"Well, is there anywhere near, where one could take about ten little girls out to tea?"

William stared at her and she went on:

"I'd better tell you the whole story, hadn't I? It sounds so odd just to ask that. . . . You see, we've just bought this house, my husband and I (my name's Mrs. Darlington, by the way). We bought it partly because our little girl's at school in the neighbourhood, and we decided to come out here to-day and have a picnic in the garden for her and her friends, though we aren't actually moving in till next month, and I'd packed a wonderful picnic basket, because I didn't want to let the child down by not doing it in style, you know, and we put it on the back of the car, and at the last minute my husband had to go up North on business, so I had to come down alone. Well, I stopped to have lunch at a hotel not very far away from here, and when I came out, the car had been stolen. *Stolen.*" She paused dramatically for a moment to let the point sink in. "I'd meant to come here quite early and get things ready, but with all the fuss about going to the police and getting a taxi, the time slipped by and I've only just got here, and now I'm here I don't know what to do. . . . I'm afraid it will let down the poor child so *terribly* for her to bring all her friends here and find nothing at all. Children never forget a thing like that. They'll always hold it against her." She paused a moment—for breath this time—then went on: "I'm really much more upset about that than about the car, because I expect the police will get it back, and anyway it's insured and we've another at home, but Sally may be here at any moment with all her friends and what *am* I to do? I was feeling just about desperate when I came in, and it was quite a relief to see someone. They always say two heads are better than one, don't they? I feel sure you'll be able to help me. Now isn't there some nice hotel I could take them all to?"

William thought over the various hostelries of the neighbourhood. They were all good sound pubs, but none of them could be described as a "nice hotel" in the sense the lady meant.

"No," he said, "but——" he glanced towards the spinney, wondering how to tell her and where to begin, when there came the sound of girlish voices—peals of laughter, exclamations of delight.

A little girl in a grey flannel coat, with a straw hat and a school hat-band, followed by a bevy of other little girls, similarly attired, came running through the spinney on to the lawn.

"Oh, Mummy, how lovely!" cried the first little girl, flinging herself into Mrs. Darlington's arms. "What*ever* made you think of it?"

"ISN'T THERE SOME NICE HOTEL I COULD TAKE THEM TO?" SHE ASKED WILLIAM.

"Of what, dear?" said Mrs. Darlington, bewildered.

"Of making a fairy feast in the little wood. It's *much* nicer than an ordinary picnic would have been. It's simply *lovely!*"

The other little girls were just as delighted. They flitted about the spinney, crying out with rapture at the cream buns half concealed in the bramble bushes,

"OH, MUMMY, HOW LOVELY! WHATEVER MADE YOU THINK
OF IT?"

the biscuits laid out on the tree-stumps, the doughnuts
hanging from the branches, the apples and bananas
on the moss by the side of the path.

Mrs. Darlington sank back into the deck-chair, pale
with bewilderment.

"I don't understand," she gasped faintly. "I
think the heat's sort of gone to my head."

William tried to explain. It was a confused explanation—all about sanctuaries and colonies, things that didn't seem to have anything to do with picnics and fairy feasts—but from it Mrs. Darlington gathered that her instinct had been right. As soon as she'd seen this boy's freckled, homely face confronting her in the garden, she'd had a feeling that he would be able to help her, and she'd been justified. She'd told him her trouble and somehow or other, by what seemed little short of a miracle, he'd managed to pull her out of the difficulty. Sally darted out of the spinney again to hug her ecstatically.

"Oh, Mummy, it was a lovely idea! They're all saying that it's the loveliest picnic they've ever been to in all their lives."

Ginger, Henry, and Douglas, who had been standing in an apprehensive group by the gate, ready to come to William's rescue if necessary, or if necessary join him in flight, had been swept up by the chattering throng of little girls, and were now accompanying them round the spinney, pointing out such of the hidden dainties as might otherwise have escaped their notice. Sally and her friends thought that Mrs. Darlington had invited them, and Mrs. Darlington thought that Sally and her friends had brought them with them, but in any case the whole party was so merry and excited that it didn't matter where they'd come from. Screams of merriment came from the spinney, where the little girls were kneeling round the bird bath lapping lemonade. . . . In the middle of the excitement a policeman arrived to tell Mrs. Darlington that the stolen car had been recovered.

"They got 'im over at Hadley," he said. "Drivin'

it cool as brass, he was. But there wasn't no basket be'ind."

"No," said Mrs. Darlington, "this little boy bravely rescued it." She had a confused vision of William's holding up the car and engaging in a desperate fight with the car-thief to secure the precious hamper for her. The policeman threw a suspicious glance at William. It was difficult, from his experience of William, to imagine him on the side of law and order.

"I know *'im*," he said, darkly.

"Yes," agreed Mrs. Darlington. "A delightful child. So serious minded. Interested in the colonial question, and things like that, and yet with such pretty ideas about fairies."

William, though he flinched inwardly at the last sentence, returned the policeman's gaze with a glassy stare, and the policeman, dismissing the problem with a shrug (always trouble of some sort where that young limb was), returned to his duties.

Tea was still in progress in the spinney, but the little girls were far too excited to eat much, and the pile of dainties had hardly seemed to diminish at all.

Then they went into the house, and William organised a game of Hide and Seek, and they chased each other up and down the back and front stairs, and clattered noisily all over the empty rooms. It was becoming just a little too rough, as games under William's direction were apt to do, when Sally suddenly discovered that it was nearly six o'clock and that they must start back for school at once.

They thanked Mrs. Darlington profusely.

"It's been the *loveliest* party, Mrs. Darlington."

"I shall *never* forget the fairy feast."

"I'm going to try to get my mummy to have a party just like it. It's the most exciting I've ever been to."

The clock struck six as the sound of their voices died away down the lane, and immediately other voices began to draw near—the sniggering, low-pitched voices of the Hubert Laneites.

"I *bet* they've not got a col'ny at all."

"They've not got food, anyway. Not the sort they said. Cream buns, I *don't* think. They've not got any money to buy 'em, an' who'd give 'em to 'em?"

"An' they'll have to s'render an' give up bein' Green shirts."

"An' we jolly well won't let 'em forget it. Yah!"

William approached Mrs. Darlington, who was leaning back in the deck-chair with her eyes closed. She opened them as William came near.

"Oh, dear!" she said. "It's been *such* a tiring day! But I'm so glad it went off so well. That fairy feast was such a marvellous idea of yours. I can't think how you managed it so quickly, either. I shall never forget how you came to my help in the crisis, my dear boy. If there's anything I can do for you in return."

"Well," said William, "there's some friends of mine outside. I wonder if I can let 'em go through that wood place——"

"The spinney?" said Mrs. Darlington.

"Yes," said William. "They're—they're sort of interested in spinneys."

"Certainly," said Mrs. Darlington. "The taxi's coming for me at half past, and I'll go straight off to Hadley to collect the car. Oh, *what* a day I've had! But you and your friends can stay here as long as you like."

"There's a lot of food left over," began William, tentatively.

Mrs. Darlington waved the food away.

"Keep it, dear, if it's any use to you. If not, just throw it away. And I shall never forget how you've helped me to-day with that charming idea of yours of a fairy feast. I'm sure it will make Sally popular for the rest of the term, and I was so terribly afraid that she'd be absolutely disgraced. She would have been if——"

But William was already opening the gate of the spinney to the Hubert Laneites.

"Come in," he said, shortly. "Here's our col'ny."

The Hubert Laneites stared till their eyes seemed in danger of dropping out of their sockets at the succulent feast that confronted them.

"You can eat as much as you like," said William generously, "an' then you can s'render an' give us up your arm things."

But the Hubert Laneites had lost their appetites—those usually hearty organs. They went along the path, their faces blank with dismay, half-heartedly eating a doughnut or cream bun, more in order to assure themselves that these dainties were real than because they had any stomach for them.

Hubert gazed through the trees at the recumbent figure of Mrs. Darlington in the chair on the lawn.

"Who's that?" he said, suspiciously.

"Her?" said William. "Oh, she's just a woman. She said she was tired an' we let her come an' rest in our col'ny. . . . Go on. Have a lap at the lemonade."

Hubert Lane put in his finger tentatively and licked it. He was disappointed to find that it really was lemonade.

c

"Now you promised to s'render an' hand us your arm things," said William.

The Hubert Laneites glanced round, obviously weighing the chances of avoiding the indignity of the proceeding by flight, but the Outlaws had closed in on them implacably, and there seemed to be nothing for it but to hand over their handsome blue armlets to William and betake themselves off as quickly as possible.

"Anyway, I was sick of the silly ole game," said Hubert, as he pulled his off, "an' I'm jolly glad I shan't have to play it again."

The others sulkily followed suit, and set off again down the lane, beginning to sing out: "Yah! silly ole Green shirts!" as soon as they were safely beyond fear of reprisals.

The Outlaws drew a deep breath of relief.

"Well, I was sick of it, too," admitted William, "but I'd rather it'd ended this way than the other."

A taxi drew up at the gate and the lady in the deck-chair roused herself from her doze.

"Oh, dear!" she said. "Is it half past already?" She looked at William and the others. "Have your friends gone, dear boy?"

"Yes," said William.

"Well, I must be going to collect my car from Hadley. You can stay here as long as you want, of course, and come whenever you like. I hope we shall see a lot of you when we come to live here. . . . I feel so grateful to you for your fairy feast, dear. I shall always think of you as the Little Boy who Believes in Fairies." An agonised spasm passed over William's face at this, but she was too short-sighted to notice it. "So kind and helpful. And so interesting—all you told me about the colonial question, though I'm afraid I don't know as much about politics as I should." She climbed into the taxi. "Now, stay as long as you like and eat up all the food. Good-bye!"

The taxi drove off, and the Outlaws were left alone. They realised suddenly that they were feeling very hungry.

"Come on," said William. "Let's get it all out on to the lawn. I'm sick of it in there since she started calling it a fairy feast."

They went into the spinney and began to collect the food, bringing it out on to the lawn—mountains of cream buns and doughnuts, pyramids of biscuits, oceans of fruit. . . . Mrs. Darlington had, in any case, provided for ten times as many guests as had arrived.

"I bet there's more'n even we can eat," said Ginger, in an awestruck voice.

"I bet there's not," said William, determinedly.

They ate contentedly and in silence, while the shadows lengthened over the peaceful garden.

William thought, with pride and pleasure, of the food-adorned spinney that had turned so strangely from a boy sanctuary into a colony, and from a colony into a fairy feast. After all, what did it matter what it was called? It had been a jolly fine idea, and it had turned out jolly well.

"Aren't the doughnuts scrumptious?" asked Ginger, his mouth full.

But the others were too busy to answer him.

CHAPTER III

AGNES MATILDA COMES TO STAY

WILLIAM knew that something was afoot in his family, but, having business of his own to occupy his mind, did not pay much attention to it. Experience had taught him that the affairs to which grown-ups attached importance were generally completely devoid of interest and not worth the trouble of investigation. Mysterious references to "little Agnes Matilda", however, finally roused his curiosity, and he decided to give the matter what attention he could spare from his own pressing and far more important business.

He sat quietly one afternoon, pretending to be buried in a book, while his mother and Ethel were talking, and, by dint of putting various twos and twos together, got the whole story more or less straight. Little Agnes Matilda was the daughter of a Mr. Warrender, an important business friend of Mr. Brown's. Little Agnes Matilda had had 'flu and had not been really well since. She could not, as her mother put it, "throw it off". She was listless and depressed. The doctor had decreed country air, but little Agnes Matilda's nurse had suddenly been taken ill and her mother was too busy to leave home. Mr. Warrender, knowing that Mr. Brown lived in the country, had asked him very tentatively if he thought his wife would be willing to take the child for a fortnight.

Mrs. Brown was not exactly eager for the company of little Agnes Matilda, but she was a conscientious wife and knew that the requests of important business friends are not to be lightly ignored. Mr. Warrender had put several good pieces of business in Mr. Brown's way, and Mr. Brown hoped that he would put several more. Little Agnes Matilda, therefore, at whatever inconvenience, must be received into the Brown household and nursed back to health and strength. The chief difficulty in the situation was, of course, William.

The Browns made enquiries among their relations to find if any of them would be willing to take charge of William for the fortnight of Agnes Matilda's visit, but there was a marked absence of enthusiasm on the part of the potential hosts. It was clear that William could not thus conveniently be disposed of. He must, therefore, be kept in the background. He must be induced to be very polite to Agnes Matilda whenever they met, but they must meet as seldom as possible.

William concurred heartily enough in this arrangement. He didn't want to have anything to do with any silly ole girl, he assured them fervently. If any silly ole girl was comin' they needn't bother tellin' *him* to keep away from her, because they all made him sick, anyway, silly ole girls did. Yes, of course he'd be polite to her. Wasn't he polite to everyone always? Well, nearly everyone an' nearly always. He would be to her, anyway. Well, was he goin' to get anythin' for it? It'd be jolly hard work bein' polite to a silly ole girl for a whole fortnight. Mrs. Brown offered threepence. William said that threepence was all right for a week, but that a fortnight was worth a jolly sight more than threepence. He'd be *extra*

polite the whole time for sixpence. And clean and
tidy and quiet? stipulated Mrs. Brown. All right,
said William. He'd throw them all in for sixpence.
Some people, he added bitterly, seemed to expect
a jolly lot for sixpence. All right, he'd stop arguin'
if she was goin' to put it down to threepence again.
He wouldn't say a single word more. He'd be polite
an' all those other things she'd said, but it was goin'
to be a jolly long fortnight. About as long as ten
years. He didn't think many people would do all
that for sixpence. It was enough to kill anyone, an'
he wouldn't be surprised if he nearly died of it. An'
all for a silly ole girl. He wouldn't mind if it'd been
for someone excitin' like an explorer or a dictator
or an engine-driver or somethin' like that, but for a
silly ole *girl.* . . . All right, all right, he was jus'
goin' out, anyway. . . .

Agnes Matilda arrived. She was worse than
William's worst fears. Even Mrs. Brown, prepared,
like a good wife, to take to her heart any child of an
important business friend of her husband's, was
disconcerted by her. Agnes Matilda was a perfect
specimen of the spoilt child. She was fat and plaintive
and disagreeable. With her arrived a lengthy time-
table of her requirements. Her meals were to be on a
lavish scale, and she had to be fed extensively between
each on broth or cocoa or milk. She had to rest
all afternoon and only take very gentle exercise in the
morning. She had to have as many sweets and
chocolates as she wanted, because they helped to
"build up her strength". She was never to be crossed
in any way. . . .

"Huh!" said William to his mother that evening. "You needn't've bothered to *tell* me to leave *that* ole girl alone. It makes me sick jus' lookin' at her."

"But you promised to be polite," Mrs. Brown reminded him, anxiously.

"Oh, I'll be that all right," said William. "She's not worth bein' anythin' else to."

As far as William was concerned, indeed, everything was quite satisfactory. He avoided Agnes Matilda most conscientiously, meeting her only at meals and treating her then with the distant hauteur of manner that was his idea of politeness.

As regards Agnes Matilda herself, things were less satisfactory. Though her appetite was excellent (in fact, she seldom stopped eating for longer than ten minutes at a time throughout the whole day), she remained pallid and listless, querulous and peevish and dispirited. She seemed to take no interest in anything. She trailed into the village with Mrs. Brown in the morning, bought as many sweets and chocolates as she required, rested and ate sweets all afternoon, and went to bed as despondent and disagreeable as she had got up. Mrs. Brown suggested various diversions, but Agnes Matilda didn't want to go anywhere or do anything. She wasn't even homesick. She didn't care where she was or what she did. She often said so in her thin, whining voice. Mrs. Brown suggested that she should give up some of her between-meal snacks, but Agnes Matilda was quite firm on that point. Her mother had said she must have them to build up her strength. . . .

The end of the fortnight drew near. Mrs. Brown would have been relieved, had it not been that, despite the country air, Agnes Matilda was still pale, listless and irritable. There was no such striking change in her as would induce a grateful father to put more pieces of business in Mr. Brown's way. William had fulfilled his part of the bargain, but somehow it hadn't helped much. . . . There was only one day left, and there was no further danger to be feared from William on that day, as he had arranged to spend it at Ginger's. Ginger's mother was going up to London for lunch and a matinée, and she had said that Ginger might invite whoever he liked for the day to keep him company. Ginger had, of course, chosen William. Mrs. Brown was much relieved by this. It meant that, at any rate, she need have no fear of his annoying Agnes Matilda on her last day. . . .

Mrs. Brown saw him safely off to Ginger's before herself setting out for the village.

Agnes Matilda had decided not to go into the village that morning, She said that she was tired of going into the village. No, she didn't want to do anything else instead. She didn't want to do anything at all. She'd just sit in the garden and eat her chocolates (a large box of chocolates had arrived from her mother by the morning's post). No she didn't want anything to read. She'd rather just do nothing. She was feeling a bit tired. . . .

Secretly glad to be relieved of her guest's company, and consoled by the knowledge that William, that potential disturber of the peace, would be at Ginger's for the rest of the day, Mrs. Brown departed to the village. For some time Agnes Matilda sat on the garden seat, eating chocolates. She was bored, but then she was always bored. She was going home

"WHAT ARE YOU FOLLOWING
ME FOR?" DEMANDED WILLIAM,
ANGRILY.

to-morrow, but she wasn't looking forward particularly
to that, because she'd be just as bored at home.

Suddenly she saw the horrid dirty little boy, who
lived there, coming in at the side gate (William had
forgotten his catapult, and had come back for it). He

entered the house, then came out again through the side gate into the road. On an idle impulse Agnes Matilda got up and followed him. She didn't know why she did it, because it was just as dull in the road as in the garden. It was just as dull everywhere. . . . She was on the point of going back to the garden when the boy turned round. His freckled, grubby face wore a stern frown.

"What you followin' me for?" he said, severely. "Go back."

"I'm not following you," whined Agnes Matilda.

"Yes, you are. An I don't want you. Go on back."

He was aware that this mode of speech hardly came under the general heading of politeness, but he understood his promise to refer only to ordinary domestic contacts beneath his parents' roof. He wasn't going to stand being followed by this awful girl in the public road. He resented everything about her—her voice, her appearance, and her obnoxious habit of eating sweets and chocolates without offering them to anyone else.

"Go on back," he ordered her again. "Haven't I told you I don't want you?"

Agnes Matilda was not accustomed to being addressed in this fashion. With Agnes Matilda one coaxed and cajoled. One did not order. She stood her ground, staring at him in amazement. He turned and went on down the road. She continued to follow him. He turned again and angrily ordered her back. She merely stared at him and, as soon as he moved on, continued to follow. Nonplussed, he decided to ignore her. She'd soon get tired of it. Anyhow, he wasn't going to encourage her by taking any more notice of her.

He had arranged to meet the Outlaws and go with them to Dean Copse, where an owl's nest had been discovered.   They were waiting for him at the corner of the road.   William approached them self-consciously, still followed by the glowering Agnes Matilda. The smiles of welcome faded from the Outlaws' faces when they saw his companion.

"What've you brought *her* for?" demanded Ginger, indignantly.

"I've not," retorted William.   "I've been tryin' to get rid of her.   It's that awful girl that's been stayin' at our house.   Don't take any notice of her.   She'll soon go back."

The gang walked on down the road, Agnes Matilda still following.   Agnes Matilda was controlling her feelings with difficulty.   Never before in her precious, petted, guarded life had she been treated like this. She, whose slightest word was listened to with loving sympathy, whose slightest wish was obeyed, was being deliberately ignored by four nasty, dirty little boys, who ought to be grateful to her for speaking to them at all.

They had stopped at a gate leading into a field.

"Bet I hit that tree," said William, drawing his catapult from his pocket.

He shot.   His shot went wide.   The three others tried with the same result.   Agnes Matilda watched, her anger conquered by interest.

"Let me have a try," she demanded.

"No, I jolly well won't," said William.   "You can go home.   We don't want you."

She turned to Ginger, who was holding the catapult. "Give it me," she said.

"No, I won't," retorted Ginger, with spirit. "You go home, same as he said. We don't want you."

Primitive emotions surged in Agnes Matilda's breast. Suddenly she launched herself on Ginger, as if the catapult itself had propelled her, biting, scratching, kicking. She was a large, powerfully-built child, and the struggle was short and victorious. In a few minutes Ginger had taken to flight to an accompaniment of roars of derisive laughter from the others. He had dropped the catapult during the struggle and William had picked it up. Agnes Matilda advanced upon William.

"Give me that," she said, shortly.

"No, I won't," said William, but he spoke without his usual confidence, and looked about him in a harassed fashion as he spoke. "It's my catapult, an' anyway," he ended weakly, "we're goin' on now."

Agnes Matilda wasted no time on him. Deep and primeval instincts had been released in her. Glorious to scratch and bite and hit and kick. One got a few knocks in return, but nothing in comparison with the wild, fierce exhilaration of the process. William, like Ginger, was at a disadvantage. He had been trained in the orthodox school of fighting. He wasn't used to opponents who pulled his hair one minute, scratched his face the next, bit his hand the next, and kicked him all the time. He, too, took to flight, but the laughter of the remaining two lacked heartiness. Before the fight William had given the catapult to Henry, who now tried without success to pass it on to Douglas. Henry was obviously next on the list. Agnes Matilda advanced upon him slowly and deliberately.

"Give me that," she said.

Henry, after a moment's silent struggle with his

dignity, during which the light of battle glowed and flickered in Agnes Matilda's eye, threw it to her.

"All right," he muttered. "Take it."

Agnes Matilda picked it up. She was obviously somewhat disappointed at having won it so easily. She'd been looking forward to two more good fights. She was just perfecting her technique, and it was annoying to be thus baulked of further practice. She felt that she hadn't really done herself justice with either Ginger or William. . . .

The Outlaws walked on down the road in a sheepish silence, followed by their unwelcome comrade.

"Wasn't much of a catapult, anyway," said William at last.

The others hastened to support this view.

"No," agreed Ginger. "The elastic'd almost gone."

"I'd meant to throw it away," said William.

"Jolly good thing it's gone," said Henry.

"*Jolly* good thing," agreed Douglas, casting an apprehensive glance behind.

Agnes Matilda was experimenting with the catapult, picking up small stones, fixing them in the elastic, and aiming at trees. Her shots went extravagantly wide of their mark. The Outlaws broke into a jeering laugh then, meeting her eye, hastily turned and went on their way.

"Let's go into the field," whispered William. "P'raps she'll go straight on down the road."

They dived through the hole in the hedge and set off across the field. A furtive glance behind told them that Agnes Matilda had also dived through the hole in the hedge and was still following them. They hurried across the field and into the next.

"Look!" said Ginger, excitedly. "There's Hubert Lane an' his gang."

Sure enough, Hubert Lane and five of his supporters were at the other end of the field. Hubert was using his blow-pipe upon several unconcerned sparrows. The sparrows evidently knew Hubert and his blow-pipe and felt themselves quite safe as long as he was actually aiming at them.

Ordinarily the Outlaws would have attacked their enemy in full force, for only last Tuesday the Hubert Laneites had hidden behind a hedge and thrown handfuls of mud at them as they passed in the road, escaping before they had recovered from the attack. But, instead of leading his followers to a glorious victory, William stood looking about him speculatively. For an idea had occured to him. How much more ignominious for the Hubert Laneites to be routed by a girl than by their legitimate foes! He waited for Agnes Matilda to come up.

"Like to go'n' see that boy's blow-pipe?" he said, carelessly. "It's a jolly fine one. Much better than any ole catapult."

Agnes Matilda was, in truth, feeling disappointed in the catapult. It hadn't hit a single thing.

"Does the blow-pipe hit things?" she asked.

"Yes. Always," William assured her. "It's jolly good at hitting things. A jolly sight better'n any ole catapult."

He approached Hubert in obviously friendly fashion.

"Hello, Hubert," he said.

The Hubert Laneites looked at him suspiciously. Overtures from William, especially after last Tuesday,

were unexpected.   They were six to four (not including
the small girl who, of course, did not count), but
even at those odds the Outlaws could do a good deal
of damage.

"We're goin' to see an owl's nest," went on William.
"Like to come too?"

Suspiciously, uncertainly, the Hubert Laneites drew
near.   After all, they *were* six to four, and an owl's
nest was an owl's nest. . . .

William turned to his followers.

"They can come with us, can't they?" he said.

Blindly following his lead, the other Outlaws smiled
with glassy friendliness.

"'Course they can," they said.

The hesitancy dropped from the manner of the
Hubert Laneites as the meaning of this sudden friendliness dawned on them.   The Outlaws, of course, were
afraid.   They'd learnt a lesson from last Tuesday.
An insolent swagger invaded their walk as they came
towards the Outlaws.

"Come on.   You show us that owl's nest an' be
quick about it," blustered Hubert.

"Yes, you hurry up or you'll get twice what you
got on Tuesday," said Bertie Franks.

The others joined in, imitating their leaders.   William
retained his glassy smile by a superhuman effort.
The agony of being polite to his foe was almost more
than he could bear.   Would that girl *never* act?
Quite suddenly she did.   Above Hubert's blustering
voice rose a shrill:

"Give me that blow-pipe."

Hubert looked at her, astonished and indignant.
How dared this representative of a despised and

"THIS DOESN'T HIT THINGS I AIM AT," SHE COMPLAINED.
"YOU'RE A STORY-TELLER."

negligible sex raise her voice, when even the Outlaws had plainly shown their fear of him?

"No, I jolly well won't," he said, "an' you can jolly well shut up or you'll get something you won't forget in a hurry."

The rest happened exactly as William had meant it to happen. It far surpassed Agnes Matilda's previous efforts. She had evidently learnt much from experience. Her onset was more sudden, her scratches

"YOU DON'T KNOW HOW TO USE IT," SAID THE OUTLAWS.

and bites deeper, her kicks more savage. In a few moments a bellowing, panic-stricken Hubert was fleeing from the scene as fast as his fat legs could carry him. His followers watched, aghast. For their leader to be defeated by a girl was bad enough, but for it to happen in front of the Outlaws was nothing short of calamity. It would be all over the village in no time. Bertie Franks had picked up the blow-pipe when Hubert dropped it, and he went rather pale as the fatal demand: "Give me that," reached his ears. He looked at the ruthlessly advancing Agnes Matilda as a rabbit might look at a weasel, then, throwing it to her with a "Take it, then," set off after his leader, accompanied by all the other Hubert Laneites. Their departure was in fact a precipitous flight, and they were sped on their way by the jeers and cat-calls of the Outlaws.

The Outlaws' feelings towards Agnes Matilda had now changed completely. They felt warmly grateful to her. They turned to her to congratulate her, as she stood there testing the blow-pipe. But she fixed them with a hard, accusing eye.

"Thought you said this would hit things," she said in an ominous voice. "Well, it doesn't."

"It will when you've had a bit more practice," William reassured her, pacifically. "Honest, it will."

"You said it would, anyway," she accused him. "And it doesn't. It hasn't hit anything I've aimed at, no more than the other thing did. You're a story-teller, that's what you are."

"Come on," said William to the others, in disgust, and they set off quickly down the road. But it was not so easy to shake off Agnes Matilda. She con-

tinued to follow them, muttering angrily to herself,
enlarging on the inadequacy of the blow-pipe and the
mendacity of William.

"Doesn't hit a single thing. A story-teller, that's
what you are. A nasty mean ole story-teller. . . .
I'm goin' to pay you out too. I'm goin' . . ."

The Outlaws slackened their pace. They had
reached the wood now. In Dean Copse their objective
awaited them—the owl's nest. It would be sacrilege,
somehow, to take Agnes Matilda to the owl's nest.
Besides, they'd jolly well stood her as long as they
could. She'd served her purpose in humiliating their
foes, and now they must, somehow or other, get rid
of her. They held a quick, whispered consultation.
Even to their rudimentary sense of honour a con-
certed attack on her was impossible, and they had
tried single combats without success. Suddenly
William's attention was caught by an old shed that
had once been used by the keepers for storing food for
game. It was never used now (except occasionally
by the Outlaws), but there was a strong and service-
able bolt on the outside.

"If we could get her in there. . . ." whispered
William.

Agnes Matilda came up to them, still harping on her
grievance.

"It's not hit a single thing I aimed at ever since I
got it," she said. "You're a mean ole story-teller,
that's what you are."

"Can't you talk about somethin' else for a change?"
said William.

"What else is there to talk about?" demanded
Agnes Matilda.

"Well, there's this shed," said William. "It's a jolly nice shed. Go in an' have a look at it."

"Go in yourself," said Agnes Matilda.

The Outlaws were nonplussed for the moment. Then William had another idea. He went to the door and called out: "Gosh! Look at this great big rat."

But there his knowledge of feminine psychology was at fault. He expected Agnes Matilda to be as fond of rats as he was, and she wasn't. Far from it. She blenched and drew back.

"All right," said William. "There isn't a rat. I was only pulling your leg. Go in an' see for yourself that there isn't a rat."

"No, I won't," retorted Agnes Matilda, with spirit. "I'm sick of the silly ole shed. Come on an' show me that owl's nest you talked about. I don't believe there is one. If it's as good as your ole catapult an' blow-pipe it'll be a rotten ole thing."

Then William had another idea—a better one this time.

"Come on in," he said to the others. "There's somethin' jolly int'restin' in there I want to show you." He turned to Agnes Matilda. "Don't *you* come in," he said. "It's a secret."

In her indignation Agnes Matilda forgot even the rat.

"I'm comin' in, too," she said, "an' if anyone tries to stop me I'll——"

She pushed her way through them into the shed, and then, to her amazement, found herself alone. The Outlaws had swiftly withdrawn. She started to follow them, but it was too late. The door was slammed, the bolt shot home. It was the Outlaws' turn to blench at the tornado of rage that filled the air—the screams and yells and threats, the pounding on the door. . . . So violent was her onset that the Outlaws almost feared the shed would collapse before their eyes.

"Gosh!" breathed William, dismayed. "I say, we can't leave her in there goin' on like that."

"Well, we can't let her out goin' on like that," said Ginger, firmly. "Let's get away quick before she breaks the whole thing down. She's more like a tiger than a yuman being."

"Yes, let's get away quick," agreed Douglas, nervously.

Douglas had not actually been attacked by the lady, but he had watched her attacking others, and it had been an awe-inspiring sight.

They hastened to Dean Copse and inspected the owl's nest. It was a good nest (in a hollow tree), but the Outlaws' interest in it was only half-hearted.

"What're we goin' to do about that girl?" said Henry at last, voicing the general feeling of uneasiness. "We can't leave her there to starve to death."

"Well, we can't let her out," said Ginger again. "She'll be awful. Worse than she was before she went in."

"Tell you what," said William. "We'll get someone else to let her out. Someone who doesn't know what she's like."

"Yes, but who?" said Henry.

"Let's have a good think," said William.

They had a good think.

"Someone brave," stipulated Ginger, breaking the silence of thought.

"Yes, they'll have to be *jolly* brave," agreed Douglas.

"I *know!*" said William, excitedly. "General Moult. He's been in a war. He's fought savages. He oughter be all right with her."

"We'd better not tell him we put her in."

"No, we jolly well won't. *Tell* you what. We'll write a note an' put it through his letter-box. Without any name, so he won't know who did it. Like what they do in books an' the pictures."

"Anonymous," put in Henry, with an irritating air of knowledge.

"Oh, shut up!" said William. "That's what we'll do, anyway. Let's go to Ginger's an' do it. His house is nearest."

They went to Ginger's, where Ginger produced a crumpled piece of paper and a pencil with an almost invisible point. Sitting on his bedroom floor, surrounded by the others, he wrote slowly and laboriously in capital letters at William's dictation:

GIRL IMPRISSONED IN HUT NEER DEEN COPS PLESE RELESE.

Then, very furtively, they all sallied out to General Moult's house. No one seemed to be about. William crept up to the front door and dropped the note through the letter-box. They could not know, of course, that General Moult had gone away for a few days, giving his domestic staff a holiday, and that the house was shut up. Then, feeling that a delicate situation had been adequately dealt with, they separated for lunch.

"She'll make a jolly fuss when she *does* get out." said William, as he accompanied Ginger home.

"Shun't be surprised to hear poor old General Moult's in hospital after it."

"Well, he's used to it," Ginger reassured him. "He's been in wars an' things. I expect he likes it."

"An' we'll get in a jolly row when she starts tellin' how we shut her in," said William, gloomily. "I bet I don't get that sixpence now. As if I could help it! I din' *ask* her to come."

"We'll pretend the wind blew the door to, an' the bolt sort of got shut in with the bang, an' that we thought she'd gone home," suggested Ginger.

"Yes," agreed William, "an', anyway, I'm not goin' home till to-night. Perhaps they'll all have forgot by then."

"Yes, an' we've got all this afternoon," Ginger reminded him. "We can go an' fish in that stream where we caught all those minnows las' week. I bet there'll be more still by now."

"Yes, an' I'll get some better worms than I had las' time," said William. "Some of 'em weren't any good at all. . . ."

They had completely forgotten Agnes Matilda by the time they reached Ginger's house.

No one would have recognised the usual listless, despondent Agnes Matilda in the small, screaming virago who flung herself again and again upon the wooden door. Oddly enough, she wasn't frightened. She was even enjoying the experience. Strange things had happened to her to-day. Instincts that had never before found outlet had found it to-day, and the excitement of it all was still upon her. She was enjoying smashing at the door and screaming, just as she'd enjoyed biting and scratching. She went on

screaming and banging the door, long after she realised
that the Outlaws had left her.   Then she sat down to
rest.   She realised suddenly that she was tired.   She'd
had more exercise to-day than she'd had for months
past.   And she was hungry.   There was no doubt at
all that she was hungry.   She'd missed her usual
allowance of sweets and the large basin of broth at
eleven, and it was long after lunch-time.   Her per-
petually over-burdened stomach realised, with surprise
and dismay, that for the first time in its life it was
empty.   Or almost empty.   And its usual state of
surfeit made the emptiness all the more unbearable.
. . .   Still, she was even more tired than hungry so,
curling up on a heap of bracken in the corner of the
hut, she went to sleep.

It was several hours later that she woke, to find
someone cautiously opening the door.   She sat up
and met the startled gaze of Fat Sam, the tramp,
who, when in that district, was in the habit of using
the little hut as a hostelry.   Of the two, Fat Sam got
by far the greater shock.   He was on the point of
quickly withdrawing and vanishing from the landscape
(for, despite his fatness, Sam could vanish from any
landscape with almost incredible rapidity) when Agnes
Matilda said:

"Don't stand there like that.   Come in."

Shorn, as it now was, of its usual listless whine, Agnes
Matilda's voice had a sharply compelling quality that
Fat Sam automatically obeyed.   He'd once had a wife
who ordered him about in that voice.   He had, in fact,
taken to the road in order to escape that voice, but the
habit of years was strong.   He entered the shed and
stood looking meekly down upon Agnes Matilda.

"What have you come here for?" she demanded.

"Well," he explained, apologetically, "it's like this 'ere. I comes 'ere when I'm roundabouts, to 'ave a rest an' a bit of somethin' to eat."

Agnes Matilda's eyes gleamed at the mention of something to eat. Her sleep, though it had refreshed her, had made her hungrier than ever.

"What are you going to eat?" she demanded.

Fat Sam drew a large newspaper package from his ancient, tattered coat. "Jus' a bit of bread an' cheese," he said.

"Come on," she said, shortly. "Sit down and let's start."

Fat Sam sat down and opened the newspaper package. It contained some crusts of hard bread and some mouldy cheese.

"We'll divide it," said Agnes Matilda, generously.

Fat Sam sighed—it had been barely enough for himself—but he knew better than to argue with that voice. Agnes Matilda divided the crusts and cheese in a businesslike fashion, then set to work with gusto upon her share. Never in all her life had she tasted anything so delicious—not even the delicacies with which at home her mother tried to coax her reluctant appetite. She finished first, then turned such a speculative eye upon what was left of Sam's that he hastily bolted it.

She took up the newspaper from the floor, searching it for crumbs, and swallowed the very last fragment before she laid it aside. She then turned her attention to Fat Sam, who had lit up a small, dirty, clay pipe.

"Where d'you live?" she demanded.

"Well, I don't live nowheres, as you might say,"

said Fat Sam after deep cogitation. "I'm on the road, like."

"Where do you sleep?"

"I don't sleep nowheres. Leastways, I sleeps in places like this when I gets the chance an' if not, outdoors under hedges an' such."

"And how do you get your food?" said Agnes Matilda. "It was *lovely* bread and cheese."

"Oh, jus' as it comes, like," said Fat Sam vaguely. "Folks gives it me or I earn a copper or two. Or I picks it up. I gets a rabbit or bit of poultry some days——"

"How?" demanded Agnes Matilda.

"Oh, I jus' takes 'em when they comes my way, like."

Proudly Agnes Matilda brought out the catapult and blow-pipe.

"I can help you get some," she said. "I nearly hit the last thing I tried. I'm a good fighter, too. I never found that out till to-day."

Fat Sam rose, stretched, knocked out his pipe and put it in his pocket.

"Well," he said, "I'll be gettin' on."

Agnes Matilda also stood up.

"Where are we goin' to?" she said.

Fat Sam looked down at her, his hand on the door latch.

"You're goin' 'ome," he said firmly, "an' I'm goin' on Marleigh way."

"No, I'm not going home," said Agnes Matilda. "I'm coming with you."

"Me?" gasped Fat Sam.

"Yes," said Agnes Matilda. "I'm going to be a

"I'M NOT GOING HOME," SAID AGNES MATILDA FIRMLY. "I'M GOING TO BE A TRAMP LIKE YOU."
"'ERE, YOU CAN'T," SAID SAM, AGHAST. "YOU'VE GOTTER GO 'OME."

tramp, too. I like it. I'd like it much better than living at home."

"'Ere, you can't," said Fat Sam aghast. "You've gotter go 'ome."

"Come on," snapped Agnes Matilda, setting out firmly from the hut. "Don't stand there talking. We'll never get anywhere at this rate."

In the Browns' household wild confusion reigned. Mrs. Brown had come back from the village to find the precious Agnes Matilda missing. Distracted, she had hunted through the house and garden and then gone out to search the village, in case Agnes Matilda had gone there after her and they had missed each other. She went into every shop to ask if anyone had seen her, but nobody had. For once, William was not suspected. Mrs. Brown had seen him set off to spend the day with Ginger before she went into the village, while Agnes Matilda lounged listlessly as usual in a garden chair. In this situation, at any rate, therefore, William could have no hand. The child must have wandered out into the road and been run over or kidnapped or—innumerable catastrophies unrolled themselves in Mrs. Brown's horrified imagination, each more terrible than the last. She was a delicate child. Perhaps she'd fainted into a pond or into a stream. Perhaps she'd wandered into the field where Farmer Jenks's bull was kept and been gored to death. Perhaps she'd fallen and sprained her ankle and was lying in some remote spot, helpless and starving. Perhaps she'd been lured away by some enemy of her father's, who would hold her up to ransom. In any case, she, Mrs. Brown, was directly responsible. The precious child had been committed to her care. . . . She was almost beside herself when lunch-time came and still the child had not returned. She'd hoped not to have to make the matter public, but now she rang up the police, the local hospital, and everyone else she could think of. She wondered whether to send for William to help with the search and finally decided not to. William meant well, but there was no doubt that his very eagerness made him more of a hindrance than a help. He got in everyone's way and propounded impossible theories and conducted investigations in a fashion that invariably still further complicated already sufficiently complicated situations. No, better leave William out of this. She herself had seen him set off for Ginger's before any of the trouble had started, so he couldn't possibly know anything about it. The nightmare afternoon wore on. Mrs. Brown, at her wits' end, would rush out to look up and down the road, then rush back in case the telephone bell rang. When it did ring and she took up the receiver with trembling hands and a sob in her throat, it was only the butcher asking whether she'd ordered seven or eight chops for to-night, and she slammed the receiver down again without answering. She had rung up Mr. Brown, and at four o'clock he arrived, pale and anxious.

"Any news?" he said.

"No, none," said Mrs. Brown, repressing a strong and natural desire for hysterics. "Heaven knows what her people will say. I suppose we ought to ring them up, but I've not had the courage."

"Yes, I suppose we ought," agreed Mr. Brown. He saw the many pieces of good business, that Agnes Matilda's father might have put in his way, turning round and making off as fast as they could in the opposite direction. "Probably the girl's only playing some prank. Let's just give her ten minutes more before we ring them up. What about William, by the way?"

"Oh, it's nothing to do with William, this time," said Mrs. Brown wearily. "William was out of the house before it happened and hasn't been back since. I wish it was William. We might do something about it, then."

"Perhaps we'd better ring up Warrender now," said Mr. Brown, turning reluctantly to the telephone.

But at that moment a car drew up at the gate and Mr. Warrender himself, red-faced and smiling, got out. Mrs. Brown sat down weakly in a chair.

"I simply can't bear it," she said. "I *know* I'm going to have hysterics."

Almost immediately Mr. Warrender entered the room, rubbing his hands together genially.

"Well, well, well, well," he said. "Forgive my barging in like this, but I was coming in this direction and I thought I'd pick the child up now. Save me coming round again to-morrow. The wife's very anxious to have her back. Nervous about her, you know. Thinks p'raps she wasn't really well enough to leave the doctor's care. A great responsibility, a delicate child. Anyway, I said I'd pick her up, if it's not inconveniencing you at all and take her home to-night. . . ."

He stopped. It occurred to him that his host and hostess were looking at him in a very peculiar way. Mr. Brown cleared his throat and began.

"Warrender, I have something——"

At this moment Mrs. Brown happened to glance out of the window. She saw at the gate a very strange couple—a large and tattered individual, obviously of the tramp species, and with him a dirty and dis-hevelled little girl. Despite the dirt and dishevelment, the little girl was obviously Agnes Matilda. Fat Sam had managed to find out from her the address where she was staying, and had determinedly brought her back to it. He thought it might be good for half a crown at least, and in any case he was sick of being bossed by her. She was every bit as bad as his wife. One minute she said he walked too fast and the next that he walked too slowly. She'd been on at him about something or other every minute since they left the hut. At first Agnes Matilda had been furious when she found that she was being brought back by a circuitous route to the Browns' house. On second thoughts, however, she had acquiesced. She had had a long and tiring day, and the thought of bed was a welcome one. It was beginning to rain and quite definitely she didn't want to sleep in a ditch. Better call it a day and return to civilisation. . . .

Mr. Warrender's back was turned to the window, and he did not see the strange sight that caused his hostess such deep emotion, or the gesture with which she called her husband's attention to it.

Mr. Brown acted with commendable promptitude. He turned to his wife with a careless: "Will you fetch Agnes Matilda, dear?" and then to his guest, "As I was saying, Warrender, I have something to show you that I think will interest you."

With that he led the innocent Mr. Warrender to a corner of the room from which the strange couple outside could not be seen and showed him a very ordinary brass ornament.

"You're interested in old brass, I believe?"

"Well, no," admitted Mr. Warrender. "You must be thinking of someone else. "It's old snuff-boxes I collect."

That launched him upon one of his hobby-horses, and he was still describing his collection of snuff-boxes when Mrs. Brown entered with Agnes Matilda. Fat Sam had been paid off and his professional tale of woe cut short, Agnes Matilda had been hastily and somewhat inadequately washed and brushed and the more glaring deficiencies of her toilet remedied.

Mr. Warrender stared at her. Her cheeks were flushed with exercise, her eyes bright with the day's excitement. She looked alert and happy—almost mischievous. Where was the pale, listless child he had left here?"

"By Jove!" he said. "This is marvellous. Marvellous. A transformation. A miracle. My wife will be delighted. Delighted." He held out his hand expansively to Mr. Brown. "My dear fellow, I am grateful to you. I can never repay you for this."

In the handclasp that followed, Mr. Brown saw all the good pieces of business turn round and fairly rush back in his direction.

While Mrs. Brown was getting Agnes Matilda ready for her journey home and packing her things, William returned, but no one took much notice of him. William was afraid that Agnes Matilda would have accused him of shutting her into the shed, but she had quite forgotten the incident. The whole day had been one of glorious adventure, of which the details were a trifle blurred in her memory. She remembered that William had had something to do with her day of adventure (she had a vague idea that he'd given her the catapult and blow-pipe), and for that she felt only gratitude. Mr. Brown, however, watched William rather thoughtfully and, when Agnes Matilda had departed with her father, still profusely grateful, drew him on to one side.

"Have you had anything to do with Agnes Matilda to-day, William?" he asked.

"Well," William temporised, "mother promised me sixpence for leavin' her alone."

"But have you left her alone?" demanded his father.

"Well, I did till to-day," said William.

"But you didn't to-day?"

"No," admitted William, "I didn't to-day. I didn't want her, though," he added. "She would come."

Mr. Brown put his hand in his pocket.

"I don't know whether your mother will give you your sixpence for leaving her alone or not," he said, "but, in any case, here's half a crown for not leaving her alone to-day."

CHAPTER IV

A QUESTION OF EXCHANGE

"THERE'S only one day left of the holidays," said William. "Let's do somethin' we've never done before."

The others looked at him with interest, then Ginger said: "We've done everythin'."

"No, we've not," said William. "I bet I could think of over a hundred things we've not done."

"I bet you couldn't," said Ginger. "We've had every possible sort of show there is, anyway."

"I bet we've not," said William.

"We've had a seaside show an' an animal show," enumerated Ginger, "an' a night club an'—an' every poss'ble other sort of show."

"We've not had television," said William triumphantly.

"Well, we couldn't have that."

"I bet we could," persisted William. "I've seen it an' it's only people's heads carryin' on—actin' an' suchlike—in a little hole. I bet we could easy make a little hole an' have our heads in it, actin' an' suchlike."

"People wouldn't pay to see it," prophesied Douglas.

"Don't care whether they do or not," said William. "It'll be somethin' we've never done before, an' it'll be somethin' to do the last day before we go back to school, an' it'll be somethin' to think of when ole

Markie's goin' on at us with all that rubbish about fractions an' decimals an' what not."

"Yes, but what'll we *do*?" asked Douglas.

"We'll do a sort of play," said William, "same as the one I saw. It was jus' heads in a sort of hole doin' a sort of play. I bet we could do one as good as that any day."

"We've done plays before an' they weren't any good," Henry reminded him.

"But we've not done a television play," said William patiently. "Not heads in a sort of hole, actin'. It's not like an ordinary play. We'll write it special."

"What'll it be about?" asked Ginger.

"We've gotter think about that," said William. "We can't do everythin' all in a minute. You've gotter have a bit of patience. I bet people what write plays don't do 'em straight off without thinkin'."

"Let's start thinkin' about it now, then."

"All right. We've gotter have a bad man an' a good man. You've always gotter have those two in a play."

"An' a girl," said Ginger.

"We're not havin' a real girl in it," said William firmly. "They mess everythin' up. One of us'll be the girl. All you've gotter do to be a girl is to put on a sort of silly look an' one of Ethel's hats. It's only heads in this sort of hole, you see. It won't matter what the rest of us looks like. I'm not goin' to be the girl," he added hastily.

"Neither am I," said Ginger, Douglas and Henry simultaneously.

"Well, we'll wait till a bit later to fix that up," said William. "Let's fix up the others now. I'll be the good man."

"I'll be the bad one, then," claimed Ginger hastily.

"Who'll I be?" said Douglas.

"You can be the good man's ole father," said William. "He thinks his son's been killed by the bad man an' he turns out alive, after all. He'd only been stunned."

"An' who'll I be?" said Henry.

"You be the policeman," said William. "He comes with the good man to rescue the girl when the bad man's got her kidnapped an' all tied up in an attic."

"Yes, but who's goin' to be the girl?" said Douglas.

It was at this moment that Violet Elizabeth Bott appeared in the doorway of the old barn. She looked at them from beneath her mop of curls.

"Can I come in?"

"No," said William sternly.

Violet Elizabeth entered and gazed round at them with a seraphic smile.

"What you doing?" she asked.

"Nothin'," said William. "You get out."

She smiled still more seraphically. Violet Elizabeth always seemed to thrive under insults and rebuffs.

"Can I play, too?" she said.

"No, you jolly well can't," said William.

"She's a girl," Ginger reminded him. "an' we want a girl."

They all looked at Violet Elizabeth, who continued to smile at them seraphically. They knew her to be unreliable, fickle and, like most of her sex, utterly unsportsmanlike, but, as Ginger had reminded them, they wanted a girl. William fixed her with his sternest frown.

"Will you do just what you're told?" he said.

"Yeth," promised Violet Elizabeth glibly. Violet Elizabeth had a lisp, which her admirers thought charming and her detractors detestable.

"Well, then, you've gotter act a girl what's kidnapped by a bad man an' then rescued by a good one."

"Ith it a tharade?" lisped Violet Elizabeth.

"No, it's not a tharade," mimicked William. "It's television."

"Whath televithun?" said Violet Elizabeth.

"My goodness! Don't you know *anythin'?*" said William.

"Yeth," smiled Violet Elizabeth. "I know loth of thingth. I bet I know ath muth ath you. I bet you don't know who dithcovered America. I do. I thaw it on a thigarette card."

"Well, never mind that now," said William hastily. "It's television we're talkin' about now."

"Wath televithun?" demanded Violet Elizabeth again.

"It's—it's head's actin' in a sort of hole," said William.

"A thort of what?"

"A sort of hole. They jus' sort of make up a tale an'—an' act it in a sort of hole."

"It thounth thilly," said Violet Elizabeth judicially.

"That's 'cause *you're* silly," retorted William. "It sounds all right to people what've got a bit of sense. They pay money for it. Lots of money. Jus' to have one of these things with heads actin' in a sort of hole."

"All right," agreed Violet Elizabeth sweetly. "What'll we act?"

"That's jus' what we're fixin' up now," said William,

"an' if we let you come in, too, you've gotter do jus' what you're told to do."

"Courth I will," said Violet Elizabeth sweetly. "I alwayth do."

Surprise at this flagrant mis-statement of fact deprived them of speech for a moment, then William said:

"Well, now we've gotter think out a story. You've gotter be the girl——"

"The heroine," said Violet Elizabeth smugly.

"An' I'm goin' to be the good man."

"The hero," said Violet Elizabeth.

"An' Ginger's bein' the bad man."

"The villain."

"An' Douglas's bein' my father. Bet you can't find a word for that," he added triumphantly. "An' Henry's bein' the policeman."

"An' whath the thory?" demanded Violet Elizabeth.

"That's what we've gotter fix up," said William.

*   *   *   *   *

The Television Show had been arranged for the following afternoon. A clothes-horse had been borrowed from Ginger's kitchen and an old sheet hung across it. A convenient hole in the middle of the old sheet had been enlarged till it could contain two heads at fairly close quarters. It was a jagged, uneven hole but, as William pointed out, would be a change from the usual square one.

A large notice had been affixed on to the door of the old barn. "TELLYVISHON ENTRANCE FREE". For, after much discussion, the Outlaws had decided not to charge any entrance-fee to their new show. The decision was due less to generosity than to a

conviction that otherwise it would not be patronised
at all. The juvenile population of the village demanded
a good deal for its money and had almost completely
wrecked the Outlaws' last show, on the grounds that
it was not worth the halfpenny charged for it.

"We'll jolly well let 'em have it free this time,"
William had said. "Then they'll have to sit quiet an'
listen, 'stead of shoutin' out for their money back."

The audience was a fair-sized one, for the Outlaws'
shows could generally be trusted to provide some little
excitement, even if not of the sort contemplated by
their organisers.

They sat here, there, and anywhere on the floor,
and stared at the jagged hole in the sheet, making
depreciatory remarks on the accommodation provided
and the probably inadequate nature of the entertainment.

Arabella Simpkin, as usual, was the chief agitator.
Arabella's mother earned her living by "obliging" the
ladies of the neighbourhood, but the social boundaries
were very sketchy among the junior inhabitants of the
village, and Arabella, by means of a forceful personality,
had dominated them from babyhood. She sat now in
the front row, holding a bag of monkey nuts, with
which she regaled herself from time to time.

She was, to-day, decked out in her best, having
"borrowed" (unbeknown to her mother) the pride
of her mother's wardrobe—a long, raggy, once-white
feather boa, always referred to by her mother as
"me fur". Arabella's mother had gone out for the
day and so was not likely to notice the absence of her
treasure. Arabella made great play with this, flinging
the long ends over her shoulder, wrapping it several

times round her neck, swinging it round and round, and to and fro.

"If it's the same sort of show they generally give," she prophesied with gloomy relish, "it'll be jolly rotten."

Arabella always came to the Outlaws' shows, and was always the first to demand her money back. She was feeling slightly aggrieved now, because the show was free and it would be impossible to make that particular protest.

There was the sound of whispered colloquy behind the curtain, then William came out and surveyed his audience with a lofty frown. He was feeling somewhat worried. Violet Elizabeth had not yet turned up. He'd had a sort of idea, from the very beginning, that she'd spoil things. Somehow she always did. She'd been the limit too, when they tried to rehearse the play, wanting to have her head in the hole all the time and hardly letting anyone else speak. . . . He wished now that they'd had a play without a heroine. It must be quite possible to think one out—all gangsters and policemen and things. The one they'd made up hadn't had much of a heroine till Violet Elizabeth got hold of it and after that it had had little else. Violet Elizabeth insisted on dominating every situation. She even insisted on staying in the hole while the villain was plotting to kidnap her.

"It dothn't matter," she said sweetly. "I'll pretend I'm not listening. I want them to go on theeing me."

And now, though it was five minutes after the time at which the performance was to have started, she hadn't turned up. It would, of course, have been a good thing to dispense with her altogether, but she'd

"I LIKE YOUR FUR," SAID VIOLET ELIZABETH, SWEETLY.

made the play so entirely her own that they wouldn't have known how to do it without her, and it was too late to make up another one. . . .

There she was at last—entering the barn door with a flourish. A sister of her mother's was spending the day with them, and Violet Elizabeth had crept into her mother's room and appropriated the hat and fur that the visitor had left on the bed. It was a small straw hat, with a flower and an eye-veil, and Violet Elizabeth wore it at a jaunty angle. The fur was a small, mink necklet. The cousin was not going home till evening and Violet Elizabeth intended to return them as soon as the Television Show was over. She had borrowed them early in the afternoon, and the reason why she was late was that she had not been able to tear herself away from the contemplation of her reflection in the mirror. The fur in particular she admired. At least, she did till she saw Arabella flinging one end of the long, feather boa over her shoulder and cracking a monkey nut at the same time. Violet Elizabeth stopped and looked at her. Suddenly she yearned with all her might to throw the end of a long fur over her shoulder. The mink necklet was no use. It was short and unthrowable. It seemed, suddenly, wholly unsuitable for a heroine. She smiled sweetly at Arabella.

"Hello," she said.

Arabella, secretly flattered, looked at her dourly and cracked another monkey nut.

"Hello," she replied ungraciously.

"I like you fur tho muth," said Violet Elizabeth still more sweetly.

Arabella looked down at it complacently and cracked another monkey nut. Then she glanced with interest at Violet Elizabeth's fur. There was an expensive look about it that appealed to Arabella. Her interest was tinged with envy.

"Yours isn't so bad," she admitted grudgingly.

Violet Elizabeth, reading aright the interest and the envy, acted promptly.

"Leth thwop," she suggested.

Arabella looked again at the mink necklet. It was small and dun-coloured, but it was the sort of thing that people wore on the pictures. It took all the glamour from the feather boa.

"All right," she said, hiding her pleasure beneath a show of indifference. "I don't mind if you want to, but mine's a much better one."

Violet Elizabeth quickly took over the long feather boa and flung the end round her neck with a flourish as she went behind the screen.

Arabella pulled her hat farther over one eye, and fastened the mink necklet at the back of her neck. She assumed an expression that was apparently one of acute nausea, but that was in reality an attempt to look like Greta Garbo.

* * * * *

The Television Show was over. It had not been an unqualified success. Violet Elizabeth and the feather boa had taken up so much room in the hole that hero, villain, policeman, and hero's father had been practically invisible. The plot was an involved one in any case, and it became still more involved in actual performance.

"It's a rotten show," commented Arabella, at the end, but she was too busy admiring her mental picture of herself in the mink necklet to make herself as disagreeable as usual.

The rest of the audience, however, compensated for this omission.

"Yes, it *is* a rotten show," they shouted, "and we'll never come to any more of your rotten shows."

"Well, listen," said William. "It wasn't meant to go like that. It was meant to go quite diff'rent——"

"There was nothin' but an ole girl throwin' a fur about. Call *that* a play?"

"Well, it was meant to be diff'rent," persisted William. "She wasn't meant to be in it all the time, same as she was. We made it up quite diff'rent. We——"

Violet Elizabeth, seeing that she was becoming unpopular with both her fellow actors and her audience, flung the end of her boa over her shoulder again and walked haughtily to the door.

"I wouldn't act for you again," she said, "not if you athked me to."

She went down to the road. A large car had drawn up there, and a man with a red, round face got out and began to make his way across the fields to the old barn. Violet Elizabeth stood and watched. He entered the barn. Curiosity fought with pride in Violet Elizabeth's breast and pride won. She didn't care who the man was or why he'd gone to the old barn. She'd never have anything more to do with any of them. She'd never act for them again—never all the rest of her life. She threw the end of the feather boa over her shoulder and set off quickly homewards. She must put Aunt Maggie's fur and hat back before *she* started making a fuss. . . . She remembered suddenly that this wasn't the fur that she had actually borrowed from Aunt Maggie and again she hesitated. Should she go back and retrieve the small brown necklet? But again pride won the day. No, she wouldn't go back there, not for anything, after the way they'd treated her. After all, a fur was just a fur. Probably Aunt Maggie herself wouldn't remember that it was a small, brown one she'd left and not a long, white one.

She entered the Hall and stood for a moment outside the door of the drawing-room, listening.

"I've never liked her," her mother was saying.

"Neither have I," said Aunt Maggie. "I never listen to servants' gossip, of course, but her cook told my house-maid . . ."

It was clear that the two were enjoying a pleasant little discussion of their mutual friends. The loss of the fur and hat had evidently not yet been discovered. Violet Elizabeth ran upstairs and laid them carefully on her mother's bed, then slowly made her way back to the old barn. Curiosity had triumphed over pride. She had decided to forgive the audience for not appreciating her acting, because she wanted to know what the big man with the round, red face was doing at the old barn.

The sound of clapping greeted her as she approached. Evidently some sort of entertainment was in progress. The audience had swelled to double the size it had been when Violet Elizabeth left it. She stood in the doorway and watched. The big man, who referred to himself in his patter as Uncle Charlie, was giving a conjuring show, and the audience was crowding round him in rapturous delight. He was just drawing a carrot from William's neck. He had already taken a goldfish in a bowl of water from Ginger's ear. The audience was wildly excited. Even Arabella had lost her usual grim expression and was watching with shining eyes and a beaming smile.

Arabella, too, had hurried home after the Television Show to replace the fur. She had remembered, suddenly, that her mother would be back from work at five, and that she might discover the loss of her fur if it were not in its usual place. Like Violet Elizabeth, she forgot the little matter of the exchange, in the hurry of the moment, and did not remember it again till she was hanging the fur on its accustomed peg in the hall. Then, like Violet Elizabeth, she decided to leave the issue to fate and to hurry back to Uncle Charlie's conjuring show. For Uncle Charlie, it appeared, was a well-known conjurer, on his way to an engagement at a music-hall in a neighbouring town. Not quite sure if he was on the right road, he had stopped his car and made his way across the field to make enquiries of the children who were assembled there. It turned out that he was on the right road and he had more than an hour in hand. It turned out, too, that there had been some sort of a show there that had been a complete failure, and that the audience was on the point of mobbing the four boys responsible. Uncle Charles enjoyed performing to children, so he leaped nimbly into the breach, sending a batch of them down to his car for his bag, and keeping the others amused with his best patter, meantime. Then the entertainment began. The most glorious entertainment that had ever been known in the village. Arabella and Violet Elizabeth, watching entranced, forgot that there were such things as furs in the world.

Meantime, Aunt Maggie was standing in Mrs. Bott's bedroom, holding the feather boa at arm's length and surveying it with an expression of frozen horror.

"My fur's been stolen," she said dramatically, "and this—*this*—left in its place."

Mrs. Bott sat down weakly on the bed and stared at her, then, on a sudden thought, hurriedly took a key from her bag, unlocked a drawer, took out a jewel

case, unlocked that, checked its contents, and sat
down again with a sigh of relief.

"That's all right," she said.

"What's all right?" snapped Aunt Maggie.

"My pearls are all right."

"I don't see what that's got to do with it."

"No, I suppose not, dear. I only meant—I don't
see how thieves can have got in."

"Of course they must have done," said Aunt Maggie.
"That fur of mine was a really valuable one, and
look—just *look*—what's been left in its place! I'm
going straight to the police about it."

"Why not ring up?" said Mrs. Bott.

"No, I'm going in person. People never really take
any notice of you on the telephone. They just put
you off."

"I'll come with you if you like, dear."

"No, thank you," said Aunt Maggie distantly.
"I prefer to see to the matter alone."

Aunt Maggie was annoyed with her sister for taking
the matter so lightly. It was a really valuable fur, and
all people could think of was their own pearls. . . .

"Just as you like, dear," said Mrs. Bott, becoming
distant in her turn.

"Where is the police station?" demanded Aunt
Maggie haughtily.

"Just beyond the Blue Lion, on the village green,
dear. . . . I'll come with you if you like."

"No, thank you."

With another outraged glare at the feather boa,
Aunt Maggie rammed her hat on her head and flounced
out of the room. As she turned out of the Hall gates
she ran into another woman who was also hurrying

along the road and not looking where she was going. It was Arabella's mother, enraged at the discovery that "me fur" had been stolen, and a nasty little brown thing left in its place.

"I beg your pardon," said Aunt Maggie graciously.

"Granted," said Arabella's mother.

"I'm afraid I wasn't looking where I was going," went on Aunt Maggie. "I'm on my way to the police station to report a theft."

"Same here," said Arabella's mother grimly. "I've 'ad me fur stolen!"

"*What!*" said Aunt Maggie. "Yours too?"

"Yes, an 'a measly bit o' rat-skin left in its place."

"But, that's just what happened to me," said Aunt Maggie excitedly. "How very odd! There—there must be some gang at work."

"Right down below me waist me fur came," went on Arabella's mother, "an' this bit o' rat-skin only just meets round me neck."

"It's most extraordinary," said Aunt Maggie, warming to her companion in misfortune. "Most extraordinary! And so odd to leave other worthless furs in their places. Perhaps it's their idea of a joke."

"Joke!" said Arabella's mother. "I'll give 'em joke."

They had reached the police station now.

Together they entered and poured out their story.

"A really valuable fur. . . ."

"Reached down past me waist. . . ."

"An utterly worthless thing left in its place. . . ."

"Measly bit o' rat-skin. . . ."

The policeman scratched his head and looked bewildered.

THE POLICEMAN LOOKED BEWILDERED. "IT MUST BE A GANG," SAID AUNT MAGGIE.

"It must be a gang," said Aunt Maggie.

"Yes, it might," agreed the policeman judicially. "Never heard of anything like it before, though."

"Leaving worthless furs in the place of valuable ones might be a sort of—you know—a sort of trademark of the gang," suggested Aunt Maggie. "I once saw a play in which they always left cards with red triangles on."

"Yes," agreed the policeman non-committally, "it might, or, on the other hand, of course, it mightn't."

"Have you had any other cases reported?"

"Not yet," said the policeman.

"There may have been other cases that haven't been discovered yet. . . . Have any strangers been seen in the village?"

"Well, now," said the policeman, with rising interest, "it's a funny thing, but I 'ave 'eard of some strangers only a minute ago. I was jus' goin' to look into it when you come along."

The story of Uncle Charlie had spread and grown. A passing conjurer had stopped his car just beyond the village and was giving a performance to the village children in the old barn. A troupe of music-hall artists had stopped their cars in the village and were giving a performance in the old barn. A whole string of caravans had stopped outside the village and their occupants (animals and all) were indulging in some kind of wild orgy in the old barn. The story had attained these final proportions by the time it reached the policeman, and he had just been about to set out on a tour of inspection when Aunt Maggie and Arabella's mother appeared.

"There's a travellin' circus about," he went on. "Gypsies an' such like. Shouldn't be surprised if it's them. The last lot of gypsies we had through took everyone's washin' off their lines in the night. . . . You say they left you worthless furs in their place?"

"Abso*lutely* worthless," said Aunt Maggie.

"Bit o' rat-skin," said Arebella's mother.

"Probably thought it'd deceive you just long enough

for them to get clear," said the policeman. "I 'spect that's what it was."

"Yes, but what are we going to *do*?" said Aunt Maggie.

"We'd better all go down there now," said the policeman. "Tell you what. You'd better go and fetch those old furs they left. That's evidence against them. I'll go down there now and you meet me there with the old furs and we'll confront them together. That'll be best. . . . It's the old barn across the fields, you know, just outside the village. Can you be there in ten minutes?"

Aunt Maggie and Arabella's mother assured him that they could.

"That's all right then," he said. "I'll meet you there."

Aunt Maggie scurried back to the Hall. Despite the loss of her precious mink necklet she was feeling pleased and excited. She seemed to be moving in the pages of one of those blood-curdling "thrillers" that so often beguiled her leisure hours. Gangs. Ramifications of crime. Wheels within wheels. International complications. . . .

Mrs. Bott came out into the hall as she entered.

"Well, dear, what do they say?" she asked.

"Oh, it *is* a gang," said Aunt Maggie mysteriously. "The police know just who's done it. We're going to confront them now. You haven't a revolver you can lend me, have you, dear? They may be desperate, you know, and stick at nothing."

No, Mrs. Bott hadn't a revolver. She suggested a poker, an Indian club, and a table-knife, but Aunt Maggie thought that they were all too undignified.

THE POLICEMAN WAS WATCHING EVERY MOVEMENT
INTENTLY.

"No, dear," she said. "I'm afraid it must be a
revolver or nothing. If you haven't a revolver it must
be nothing, and I must just hope for the best. If the
worst should come to the worst, my will's in the
second drawer of my bureau, on the left-hand side,
underneath the tea-cosy I'm making for Aunt Fanny's
birthday. And now, dear, I must fly."

"NOW WATCH VERY CAREFULLY," SAID UNCLE CHARLIE.

Aunt Maggie ran upstairs, snatched the feather boa from the bed, and ran downstairs again.

"Good-bye, dear," she called, as she vanished from sight down the drive. "If I don't return within an hour, I think you'd better get into touch with Scotland Yard."

She hurried down the road, the feather boa fluttering in the breeze. The old barn was plainly visible from the road, and she soon found her way to it and stood, panting and breathless, in the doorway. At the farther end, in the middle of a crowd of children, was a large, fat man. His sleeves were rolled up and he was showing his audience his open hand, turning it round about to prove that there was nothing in it.

"Nothing there, ladies and gentlemen," he said. "Watch my every movement. No possibility of deception. . . . Now, I'm going to cover my hand with this handkerchief. Nothing in the handkerchief, notice."

Aunt Maggie turned her head and saw that the policeman stood near her. His eyes were fixed on Uncle Charlie's handkerchief. His mouth hung open. He was watching every movement intently.

"Now watch me very carefully," went on Uncle Charlie. "I cover my hand with the hand-kerchief. . . ."

Aunt Maggie turned in the other direction and saw Arabella's mother—the precious mink fur held carelessly in one hand. Her eyes, too, were fixed eagerly on Uncle Charlie's handkerchief. . . .

"Well, I *never!*" said Aunt Maggie indignantly, snatching the fur.

Arabella's mother glared at her, then snatched suddenly at the feather boa.

"Well, of all the *sauce!*" she said.

"Watch—very—carefully," said Uncle Charlie.

Both Aunt Maggie and Arabella's mother hastily turned to him again. The policeman was standing, his mouth still wide open, his eyes, fixed on the hand-kerchief, nearly starting out of his head.

There was a tense silence in the barn.

Uncle Charlie slowly removed the handkerchief.

A white mouse sat upon his palm and trimmed its whiskers.

"Coo!" said the policeman. "Isn't it wonderful?"

He suddenly saw Aunt Maggie and Arabella's mother.

"Well, about them furs," he began.

They turned on him indignantly.

"Be quiet," they said. "He's just going to do another."

He stared at them in astonishment for a moment, then abandoned the problem, and all three settled down happily to enjoy Uncle Charlie's next trick.

CHAPTER V

AUNT FLORENCE AND THE GREEN WOODPECKER

"I FEEL jolly sorry for them," said William thoughtfully. "They have such a rotten time."

"Who do?" said Ginger indistinctly, through a mouthful of roast chestnut.

"Grown-ups," said William. "Jus' think of the dull things they eat an' the dull things they do. Rice puddin' an' bread an' butter, an' goin' into towns an' lookin' at shops. . . ."

"Well, it's their own faults," said Douglas, manœuvring a chestnut out of the fire with a stick, taking it up in his fingers, and dropping it with a yell. "Gosh, it's hot!"

"Course it is," said Henry. "What d'you expect? Roasted chestnuts nachrally are hot."

"Roasted moose," William corrected him.

"Yes, roasted moose," agreed Henry, remembering their rôle of Red Indians.

The four were sitting round a fire in the wood, roasting chestnuts and pretending to be a tribe of Red Indian braves under the leadership of "Hawk Eye", who was, of course, William. At first they had kept religiously to their rôles, discussing raids on neighbouring Palefaces and keeping a sharp look-out for their enemies, but they were now gradually returning to their normal character.

"It's their own faults," repeated Douglas. "They needn't go on an' on bein' so dull an' doin' such dull things."

"Yes, but they can't help it," said William, "an' that's why I feel so sorry for them. Whether it's their own faults or not, they have a jolly dull time. You can't say they don't."

"Yes, I know they do," said Douglas, "but I don't see that we can help 'em, anyway. 'Cept, of course," he added, "by bein' jolly diff'rent ourselves when we grow up."

"Yes, we'll be that all right," said William emphatically. "We'll jolly well be that all right. But I feel sorry for 'em now. I'd like to do somethin' for 'em now."

"P'raps they like bein' dull," suggested Henry tentatively.

"They can't," said William. "No one can like bein' dull."

"Well, *we* can't do anythin'," said Douglas again, emphatically.

"I don't see why we can't," said William. "I'd like to try an' give 'em a good time. Some of 'em, anyway. Some of 'em don't deserve a good time. What about havin' a Society for Givin' Decent Grown-ups a Good Time?"

The others considered this doubtfully.

"I dunno," said Ginger at last. "They're always so jolly ungrateful when you do anythin' for them."

"Yes, they are, too," agreed Douglas in a heartfelt tone. "That time I tried to clean the chimney 'cause the sweep didn't turn up, they were all *mad* at me 'stead of bein' grateful. They're all like that. An' I don't see we can change 'em."

But, as usual, William, having got hold of an idea, did not like to let it go. "I don't mean givin' 'em *all* a good time," he persisted. "I mean jus' the decent ones."

"There aren't any," said Ginger gloomily. "They're all awful. They go on an' on an' on an' *on* at you for nothin' at all. Why, jus' 'cause I happened to go through some glass in the cucumber frames when I was practisin' walkin' on the edge . . ." He left the sentence unfinished.

"Yes, they're all like that," sighed Douglas.

"Well, what'll we do now?" said Henry. "We've finished the chestnuts—I mean the moose. Shall we go'n' have a hunt for ole Fat Face?"

For years the Outlaws had constituted themselves a Red Indian band under William's leadership, and Hubert Lane, their ancient enemy, had taken no interest in the proceedings, but recently an aunt had presented him with a Red Indian suit, complete with magnificent head-dress, and, on the strength of this, he had organised his followers into a band of braves under his leadership, taking the name Lion Face, which the Outlaws had corrupted to Fat Face. They roamed the woods, but seldom met William's band, for Hubert was always more adept at evading than at meeting his foes. Ocassionally William and his band would amuse themselves by "hunting ole Fat Face" and chasing him and his braves out of the wood, but generally they were content to let them go their way. There was no doubt at all of the supremacy of Chief Hawk Eye, and there the matter was allowed to rest.

"No," said William, "I'm tired of chasin' ole Fat Face. He never does anythin' but run away anyway, an' even then he's so easy to catch that it isn't any fun."

"What'll we do, then?"

At that point an angry shout in the distance warned them that a keeper had seen the smoke of their fire.

"Palefaces!" said William, springing up. "Come on. Let's pretend to run away, an' lead them into an ambush."

With this ruse for "face-saving", the Outlaws ran as fast as they could out of the wood and didn't draw breath till they reached the old barn. There they sat down on the ground, panting.

"He nearly got us that time," gasped Ginger.

"Yes, it was the thin one," said Douglas. "He runs quicker than the other."

"We won't give either of *them* a good time when we've got our Society goin'," said William. "We'll be jolly careful who we give a good time to."

"Well, what'll we do now?" said Henry, who wasn't particularly interested in William's Society for the amelioration of the lot of grown-ups. "Let's think of somethin' new."

The village clock struck one.

"Time for lunch," said Douglas. "We'll think of somethin' this afternoon."

After lunch Ginger had the brilliant idea of playing at smugglers and coastguardsmen in a neighbouring disused quarry, and the next day they were busy holding a review of a fleet of paper boats in the stream, so that William would have completely forgotten his proposed Society if it hadn't been for the arrival of Aunt Florence.

He had known for some time, of course, that Aunt Florence was coming to stay at his home, but he had taken little interest in the fact. He realised that aunts' visits were one of life's necessary evils, and the best way of dealing with them was to make oneself as unobtrusive as possible while they were in progress.

Aunt Florence seemed at first just like any other aunt. She was thin and short-sighted and absent-minded, and wore the style of hairdressing and coat and skirt that William had come to associate with aunts. It wasn't till the evening of the first day of her visit that William realised she was different. For, just as he was going to bed, she took out her purse and handed him two half-crowns.

"A little tip for you, dear boy," she said, with her bright aunt's smile. "I'm sure you'll find some good use for it."

William was deeply touched, not so much by the tip (which was an accepted part of an aunt's visit), but by the fact that it was given on the first day instead of the last. The thought of the tip generally hung over the whole visit—imparting to it a nerve-racking atmosphere of mingled hope and fear. It was tacitly understood that the amount would depend on his behaviour. He was expected to earn it by excessive politeness and an almost impossible perfection of deportment. A series of misunderstandings could reduce it from the expected five shillings to a shilling or even sixpence. It had been known to vanish altogether. . . . That an aunt should deliberately put an end to this painful state of suspense, by giving her tip on arrival instead of on departure, was un-precedented, and, as I have said, it touched William deeply. Moreover, it focused his attention upon her. He felt that he would like to express his gratitude to her in some tangible form.

At first there didn't seem to be any way in which he could do this. They had, it turned out, few, if any, interests in common, for Aunt Florence was one of those bird enthusiasts for whom William had so little sympathy. As if the world wasn't full of things infinitely more interesting than birds! There were rats, for instance, and frogs and weasels and tadpoles and spiders and rabbits and lizards. The undue im-portance assigned in the animal creation to birds by elderly maiden ladies had always irritated William. Bird baths and bird tables! Nuts and crumbs and bits of cake! As if nothing but birds ever wanted anything to eat! William was sorry to find that Aunt Florence belonged to this class, but she definitely and outstandingly did. She had a little "bird diary", in which she noted down all her observations, together with date and place. She imitated the notes of birds in a shrill falsetto. Unaware of William's deep-rooted prejudice against this hobby, she even tried to interest him in it.

"The bird I particularly want to find, William," she said earnestly, "is a green woodpecker. It makes a noise like this." She opened her mouth and emitted a shrill, short peal of laughter. "Curious, isn't it? If ever you hear it, do let me know. I've been trying to find one for years. Literally years. It would be such a joy to me to find one here."

William concealed his disgust as best he could, for

the fire of gratitude still burnt fiercely in his heart. To give him five shillings on the very first night, without waiting to see if he was going to be polite or anything!

"Poor ole thing!" he said to his Outlaws. "She has a jolly rotten time. Nothin' but birds an' things like that. It's the same with all grown-ups, one way or another," he went on, returning to his theme.

"I bet you anythin' they like bein' dull," said Henry again.

"They can't," said William firmly. "Not as dull as that. No one could. It's just that they've forgotten how to have a good time. I bet they'd enjoy it as much as anyone, if only they could get back into the way of it. . . . Birds!" He made a grimace expressive of deep disgust and emitted an exaggerated imitation of the green woodpecker note, as rendered by Aunt Florence. "They can't like bein' as batty as that. I bet if someone took the trouble to give them a jolly good time, same as they used to have when they were children, they'd enjoy it, and it'd start 'em bein' jolly again, an' they'd never want to go back to bein' dull. An' I bet we start on her. She deserves it. She was jolly decent about that tip. An' she mus' have an awful time."

"Well, I don't see how you're goin' to do it," objected Ginger.

"I don't either, jus' at present," admitted William, "'cause she's goin' about with my mother all the time, an' I know it wouldn't be any good tryin' to make my mother jolly. I'll jus' have to wait an' see how things sort of go on."

After tea he rejoined them in a state of great excitement.

"I say!" he said breathlessly. "I bet it'll be all right to-morrow. My mother's gotter cold an' is goin' to stay in bed to-morrow an' my aunt'll be by herself. I bet we can give her a jolly good time if she's by herself. There won't be anyone to interfere an' make her do dull things. I'll get her straight after breakfast an' start givin' her a jolly good time. Well, I'll start before that. I'll give her a jolly good breakfast—not the dull sort of stuff grown-ups gen'rally have. I'll spend some of the five shillin's on her. She deserves it. She was jolly decent to give it to me when she did. She always has her breakfast in bed, so I bet I can manage that part all right."

The next morning he intercepted the housemaid as she was coming through the hall with Aunt Florence's breakfast tray.

"I'll take that up," he said, "so's to save you trouble, 'cause you've got mother's to take up, too, this mornin', haven't you?"

He rather overdid the politeness of his voice and manner, and she looked at him a little suspiciously, but it was a busy morning, and she *had* Mrs. Brown's breakfast tray to take up as well, so she handed it to him with a cautionary: "Well, you mind what you're doing with it, that's all, and don't go dropping it all over the place."

"Me?" said William distantly. "I don't know what you're talking about. I never drop things."

"Oh, no, you don't, do you?" teased the housemaid. "Quite the lily-white hen, aren't you?"

William pulled a face at her, she pulled one back

at him, and they parted on friendly terms—the housemaid to prepare Mrs. Brown's breakfast tray, William
to carry Aunt Florence's upstairs. He paused when
he reached the landing, looked carefully round, then
vanished into his own bedroom with the tray. A
moment later he emerged and carried it into Aunt
Florence's bedroom.

"Good morning, Aunt Florence," he said kindly.
"I've brought your breakfast."

"Good morning, dear boy," said Aunt Florence,
sitting up in bed and smiling brightly. "How kind
of you! I believe I heard a chiff-chaff a minute or
two ago. I . . ."

Her voice died away as her eyes fell upon the
contents of her breakfast tray. The coffee, bacon,
toast and marmalade placed upon the tray by the
housemaid had disappeared, and in their place was a
large and unwholesome-looking bun, filled with butter
cream and decorated on the top with strips of pink
coconut, a saucerful of liquorice allsorts, a cupful of
sherbert and a carton of ice-cream that had returned
to its liquid state during the night. She looked up in
amazement, but William, having presented his offering
of dainties, had modestly retired. She looked down
again with increasing bewilderment at the tray. It
must, of course, be some special diet. Really, the
modern craze for diets was ridiculous. She'd come
across a good many strange ones—at the last place
where she'd stayed they'd all started the day with
raw carrots—but this was the oddest she'd ever met.
Fortunately, she never ate much at breakfast in any
case, and she had a tin of plain biscuits with her.
She always carried a tin of plain biscuits about with

her. She'd found them very useful at the raw carrots place. She ate two or three, then poured away the sherbert and liquid ice-cream, so as not to seem too unappreciative, and got up and dressed.

After that she came downstairs, sat down by the dining-room window and opened the newspaper.

Meantime, upstairs, William hastily returned coffee, bacon, and marmalade to her breakfast tray, noting with approval that the sherbet and the ice-cream had disappeared, and pocketing the bun and liquorice allsorts so that they shouldn't be wasted. Evidently she'd enjoyed the sherbet and ice-cream, at any rate. Perhaps one couldn't expect a grown-up to get into the way of having a good time, all at once. It would have to come gradually. . . . He went downstairs again. Aunt Florence looked up from her newspaper.

"I thought I'd go down to Hadley and look at the shops this morning, William," she said brightly. "Such a pity your dear mother can't come with me."

He looked at her pityingly, wondering again why grown-ups endured such agonies of boredom when they might be doing something really interesting. Well, Aunt Florence, at any rate, was to be saved from it. She was going to do something really interesting.

"I can come along with you," he said.

"Very well, dear," said Aunt Florence. "That's very nice of you. We'll set out at once, shall we?"

She chattered brightly, as they walked down the road.

"Of course, the fly-catcher comes back later than most of the birds and, unlike many of the others, he uses his old nest. The green woodpecker, the one I was telling you about, that I'm so very anxious to

E

"I'M DELIGHTED TO MEET YOU, DEAR BOYS," SAID AUNT
FLORENCE.

see, frequents open country as a rule, rather than
woodlands and . . ." She stopped. William was
turning from the road into a side lane. "Surely
this isn't the way to Hadley, dear boy!"

"Yes, it is," said William, and qualified the statement by adding, "sort of", assuring himself at the
same time that everywhere was the way to Hadley
in the sense that you could get to Hadley from it.

"Well, anyway, it's very pleasant," said Aunt

"WE THOUGHT P'RAPS YOU'D LIKE TO HAVE A GAME OF
RED INDIANS WITH US 'STEAD OF GOING INTO HADLEY,"
SUGGESTED GINGER, TRYING TO LOOK ENTHUSIASTIC.

Florence. William opened the gate for her to enter
the wood. "Very pleasant indeed. Quite a bird
sanctuary, I've no doubt. I might even see a green
woodpecker here."

William sighed. It was certainly high time she
had something else to think about than green wood-
peckers. Well, after this morning she would have. . . .

They walked down the path till they came to the
little clearing where Ginger, Henry and Douglas were
waiting for them.

"Dear, dear!" said Aunt Florence. "Who are these?"

"They're just friends of mine," explained William. Aunt Florence beamed at them.

"Delighted to meet you, dear boys," she said.

"We thought p'raps you'd like to have a game of Red Indians with us, 'stead of goin' into Hadley," suggested William persuasively.

For a moment Aunt Florence looked slightly taken aback, then she rallied her forces. It was, after all, a compliment to be asked to play with the dear children.

"Well, yes, dear, for a few minutes, perhaps," she said. "It's a delightful spot—is it not?—and will give me an opportunity of watching my feathered friends. Er—how do you play the game, dear boys?"

"Well," explained William, "this bush is our wigwam, an' we're four braves an' you can start by bein' our squaw. You can be called Shining Water. That's a good squaw name. We're goin' out huntin' now an' you're stayin' here to look after the wigwam an' be ready to cook the moose what we bring home."

"Er—I see," said Aunt Florence brightly. "Yes, I see. That will be quite all right, dear children. I'll sit here on this tree-stump and look after the—er—wigwam. I may, of course, with luck, see a green woodpecker. . . ."

William sighed. It was going to be no easy task to educate Aunt Florence to a sense of true values. Still, he hoped for the best. He meant to initiate her very gradually into the real joys of life.

"You see," he explained to the other three, as soon as they were out of earshot of her, "if she starts by

jus' bein' a squaw she can get into the rest of it gradual,
till she sudd'nly finds she's enjoyin' it, same as she
enjoyed her breakfast this morning, an' then she'll
see how silly all that bird stuff an' lookin' at shops is,
an' start enjoyin' herself prop'ly, an' then it'll sort of
spread to the other grown-ups."

The others looked a little doubtful—they were not
blessed with William's glorious optimism—but they
thought the experiment well worth trying.

"How long'll we leave her there?" said Ginger.
"Shall we go'n' hunt ole Fat Face? We've not done
it for quite a long time. We don't want him to forget
we can lick him."

"No," said William, "we don't want to stay away
long enough to hunt ole Fat Face jus' now. We
don't want to leave her too long bein' a squaw, case
she gets tired with it. We'll go back in a minute an'
fetch her an' take her out huntin' with us, an' I bet
she'll get so excited with it, she'll never want to look
at a bird or a shop again. Come on. Let's go back
now. She'll have got used to bein' a squaw, an' it'll
be time to start her on the next part. We'll make her
a chief after we've been out huntin' a bit. What'll
we call her?"

After some discussion, it was decided to give Aunt
Florence (who was notoriously short-sighted), the
somewhat incongruous name of Eagle Eye, then they
set off briskly towards the wigwam. And there they
had their first shock. For Shining Water had disappeared, and on the empty tree-stump, where she
had been sitting, was a piece of paper on which was
written: "We've capchered your squaw. Yah—Lion
Face."

The Outlaws stared at it in consternation. The hated and despised Lion Face had carried off their squaw. And the great question was, where had he carried her to?

"Let's hunt all through the wood," suggested Ginger. "Let's sep'rate into twos an' go diff'rent ways an' then when we've found where she is, we can join up an' rescue her."

"No," said William. "I bet she's not in the wood at all. I bet they wouldn't dare keep her in the wood 'cause they'd know we'd find her an' jolly well bash 'em up. I bet he's taken her to his house, 'cause he'll think we won't be able to get in there. Let's go there quick an' see, anyway."

They ran down the path to the road and along the road to Hubert Lane's house. And there, through the hedge, they saw the innocent Shining Water in the drawing-room, engaged in polite conversation with Hubert's mother.

Aunt Florence had taken for granted that her capture was part of the game, and had acquiesced in it without protest—even with alacrity, when she saw that it was ending in a comfortable chair in a civilised drawing-room. She had at first refused the invitation to lunch that Mrs. Lane had given her at Hubert's earnest request, but her refusal had been easily overcome and a message to that effect had now been despatched to the Browns' house.

"I've had quite a busy morning," she was saying brightly. "Playing Red Indians with the dear children. My nephew and your dear little boy invented quite an exciting game for me, including a capture. I'm so fond of children and it's so nice to

"YOU GIVE US OUR SQUAW BACK," DEMANDED WILLIAM.
"WE JOLLY WELL WON'T," SAID HUBERT, "SHE BELONGS
TO OUR TRIBE NOW."

feel that I've given them a little pleasure, though
really, of course, I'd meant to go into Hadley. . . ."

William and the Outlaws cautiously tried the gate.
It was bolted. William was just beginning to climb
over it when Hubert and his gang appeared, coming
out of the side door of the house. Hubert wore his

elaborate Red Indian costume, and was grinning derisively.

"If you climb over," he threatened, keeping a safe distance, "I'll send *him* after you."

He pointed to the gardener, who was working at the other end of the lawn. He was a large, muscular man, and the Outlaws had for him a deep respect, born of bitter experience.

"Well, you give us our squaw back," demanded William ferociously.

"No, we jolly well won't," said Hubert. "She's ours now. She belongs to our tribe. We've captured her."

"I know you've captured her," said William, "but she doesn't belong to your tribe. She belongs to ours."

"No, she's goin' to have lunch with us," said Hubert triumphantly, "an' then she'll belong to our tribe. When you've broken bread with someone you b'long to their tribe."

"Well, she's not goin' to have lunch with you," said William. "'Cause she's stayin' with us an' she's comin' home to lunch. They're expectin' her."

"She's sent a message to say she's havin' it with us," jeered Hubert. "Yah, boo! Your ole aunt belongin' to our tribe! How'll you like *that*?"

The others took up the cry, shouting: "Yah, boo! Your ole aunt belongin' to our tribe!"

"You let us come in an' speak to her," demanded William.

"No, I jolly well won't," said Hubert, "an' if you try'n' come in, we'll call *him*."

The gardener cast a morose eye in their direction. He hated boys and welcomed any opportunity of getting even with them. Hubert and his friends, of course, were sacrosanct—to touch them would mean losing his job—but he enjoyed working his grudge off on the Outlaws.

"We've—we've gotter message for her," said William desperately. "It's an important one. You'll have to let us come in to her if we've got an important message."

"No, I jolly well won't," said Hubert.

"All right," said William, "we'll do without." He lifted up his voice and yelled: "Hi! Aunt Florence! Aunt *Florence!*"

The other Outlaws joined in, shouting: "Aunt Florence. Aunt *Florence!*" at the tops of their voices.

But the Hubert Laneites began to shout, too, drowning the words in a wild, indistinguishable hubbub.

"It's just the children playing in the garden," explained Mrs. Lane in answer to Aunt Florence's startled look of enquiry.

"The dear children!" murmured Aunt Florence. "So high-spirited and light-hearted. Such *joie de vivre!*"

"It's jus' lunch-time now," Hubert said when the Outlaws at last gave up the attempt to attract Aunt Florence's attention, "an' after then she'll be always a member of our tribe, an' we jolly well won't let you forget it."

The sound of a gong came from the house.

"That's lunch," went on Hubert, "an' now you can jolly well think of her b'longin' to our tribe. For always an' always. Your ole aunt a member of our tribe. . . . *Yah!*"

With that, he vanished into the house, stopping, evidently, to warn the gardener to guard the gate. The gardener stayed working on a border near it, throwing baleful glances occasionally at the four Outlaws, as if longing for them to give him an opportunity to use his powers of guardianship on them. The Outlaws discussed the situation in whispers. There was no doubt at all in any of their minds that they would be disgraced for ever if their captured squaw broke bread in the rival chieftain's household. It would unite them by a shameful tie to their bitterest foe. It would give their enemies a handle against them for months to come. It would form a taunt to which they would have no reply. Their squaw a member of Fat Face's tribe! It wasn't to be endured.

"Look!" said Ginger. "They're goin' into the dinin'-room. I can see 'em."

"Let's try shoutin' again," said William.

Once more they raised their voices and yelled: "Aunt Florence! Aunt *Florence*!"

But evidently Hubert explained their shout of warning as one of friendly greeting, for Aunt Florence came to the window, accompanied by Hubert, and waved her hand in their direction, smiling her vague, short-sighted smile.

"So high-spirited," she murmured again, fondly. "So full of life."

"Well, that's no good," said Ginger, as she turned away, still smiling amicably, towards the table.

"They're sittin' down now," said Douglas, craning his neck. "They're jus' goin' to begin. They . . ."

And suddenly William had an idea.

Crouching down behind the hedge, he uttered the

high-pitched laugh that had been Aunt Florence's
rendering of the note of the green woodpecker.

Aunt Florence, in the act of rasing a piece of her
dinner-roll to her lips, suddenly froze into immobility.
Then she replaced her piece of roll on her plate. There
was a strained, intent look on her face as she sat there,
listening. The note was repeated. Aunt Florence
rose from her seat.

"Do you mind if I just step out into the garden?"
she murmured. "I thought I heard . . . I won't
be a moment."

Like one in a trance, she went out to the garden and
stood there, motionless, listening. The sound was
repeated. It seemed to come from the road now.
She went to the gate. Two boys were there (Ginger
had been despatched to Mrs. Brown's household to
tell them that Aunt Florence would be home for lunch,
after all). They looked rather like the boys she'd been
playing Red Indians with in the wood, but she couldn't
be sure. All boys looked more or less alike to Aunt
Florence. . . . The sound came again. Yes, it
definitely came from down the road now.

"Er—have you happened to notice a—a sort of
green bird about here?" she said to one of the boys.

"Yes," said Douglas. "I saw a green bird only a
minute ago in the hedge down there."

He pointed down the road in the direction of
William's home and quieted his conscience by the
reflection that he had actually seen a greenfinch in
the hedge, not so long ago.

The note was repeated. It was unmistakable, and
it seemed to come from farther off now. Panic swept
over Aunt Florence. Suppose she missed it now that

it was at last so near her. . . . Forgetting everything else in the world, she opened the gate and set off down the road in the direction of the sound. William, on the other side of the hedge, kept just in front of her, crouching in the ditch and uttering the note at intervals. Aunt Florence plunged along, peering into the hedge, then hurrying on at each fresh note. The note drew her on . . . down the road . . . and at last into a garden that she recognised as her hosts' own garden. The note seemed to draw her along the path to the door, then stopped, and, while she stood, waiting uncertainly, the housemaid came out and said:

"Lunch is just ready, miss."

Aunt Florence realised suddenly that she was tired and hungry. The woodpecker must have flown away. Its note had ceased entirely. It was disappointing, but, at any rate, she'd heard it quite clearly, and once or twice she could have sworn that she'd seen a flutter of something in the hedge. She thought that perhaps it wouldn't be unduly stretching the truth if she wrote: "Heard and saw green woodpecker," in the bird diary.

She entered the dining-room and sat down at the table. William was its only other occupant. His face was bland and expressionless. She remembered that she'd been playing Red Indians with him earlier in the morning.

"Have you had a nice morning, dear?" she said in her bright aunt's voice, as she passed him a chop.

"Yes, thank you," said William.

Suddenly she remembered something, and an expression of dismay came over her features.

"But, dear me!" she said. "I was having lunch

at the Lanes', wasn't I?" She looked at the house-maid, who was handing her the potatoes. "Didn't I send a message that I wouldn't be in to lunch?"

"Yes, miss," said the housemaid, "and then you sent another that you would."

She looked rather anxiously at Aunt Florence, remembering the untouched bacon and the remains of sherbet and ice-cream on her breakfast tray. Was the old josser going crackers?

Aunt Florence knit her brows.

"Did I?" she said. "I suppose I must have done. I don't quite remember. It's been such a confusing sort of morning. I meant to go to Hadley, but stayed playing with the dear children. . . . Well, perhaps you'd be good enough just to ring up Mrs. Lane and tell her that I'm very sorry not to have been able to have lunch with her, after all. Just to be on the safe side, in case she's expecting me. Tell me, dear boy," she turned to William. "Did you hear that note I was telling you about this morning? The green woodpecker's note?"

William appeared to search his memory.

"Yes," he said at last. "Yes, I *did* sort of hear that noise."

"So did I, dear boy," said Aunt Florence trium-phantly. "And, what's more, I'm almost sure I saw it."

Half an hour later, William met the other Outlaws in the old barn.

"It's all right," he said. "She didn't go back, an' she's goin' home to-morrow, so she won't be able to go there again, so it's all right. But," bitterly, "I'm jolly well never goin' to try to give another grown-up a good time as long as I live. They don't know what to do with it when you do give it 'em."

In her bedroom, Aunt Florence was wrestling with her conscience over her bird diary. At last she wrote:

"Distinctly heard note of green woodpecker. *Think* I saw it, but, owing to short-sightedness, cannot be *quite* sure."

CHAPTER VI

WILLIAM AND THE EBONY HAIR-BRUSH

"ROBERT'S had an eb'ny hair-brush for a birthday present," said William.

The Outlaws, having nothing particular to do, were willing to while away their time by discussing even this trivial subject.

"What's eb'ny?' said Ginger.

"It's a sort of black wood," said William.

"There isn't such a thing as black wood," objected Ginger. "Wood's brown, same as dining-room tables, or white, same as kitchen tables. There isn't any other sort."

"Yes, there is," said William. "There's eb'ny."

"I 'spect it's brown wood painted over black," said Douglas.

"No, it's not," said William. "It's black wood. It's eb'ny."

"It can't be. Who's ever heard of an eb'ny tree?" said Ginger.

"Go on, then. Show it us," said Henry.

"How can I?" said William testily. "It's in Robert's bedroom, an' he'd make an awful fuss if I took you in."

"Who gave it him?"

"That girl at The Lilacs. Sheila what's-her-name."

"Barron," supplied Henry.

"Yes, that's it. Sheila Barron. They've only jus' gone to live there."

"I know," said Ginger sorrowfully. The Lilacs, like most empty houses in the neighbourhood, had been a happy hunting-ground for the Outlaws before Mr. Barron and his family had moved into it. "D'you remember how we used to get in at the window over the v'randah roof, an' play highwaymen up an' down the staircases?"

"We got jolly good at climbin' up that v'randah an' openin' that window with a penknife," added Henry, in wistful, reminiscent vein.

"I bet burglars have a jolly time, getting into empty houses, an' such like," said William. "I've often thought I'd have a try when I'm grown up. That, or bein' a detective. I never can make up my mind which have the most fun, burglars or detectives."

The Outlaws, however, had discussed this subject so often that there was nothing left to say about it, so they returned to the ebony hair-brush.

"Why did she give him a hair-brush?" said Douglas. "I'd be jolly mad if anyone gave me a hair-brush for a birthday present."

"He wanted it," said William. He spoke sadly, as one deploring the degeneracy of a fellow creature. "He's batty, but they're all batty that way, are grown-ups. The things they give each other for presents make me sick! Hair-brushes an' ties an' handkerchiefs an' such like! Why, my mother asked my father to give her a set of saucepans for a Christmas present last year! *Saucepans!*"

"Did Robert ask this girl to give him a hair-brush?"

"Not 'zactly, but he saw her father's once, when

he was there, an' he said what a fine one it was, an' so now she's sent him one jus' like it for a birthday present. She's batty, too. They're all batty. An' now he's goin' about all cock-a-hoop jus' 'cause he's got a rotten ole eb'ny hair-brush. I gave him a jolly good whistle, what I'd made myself, an' he hardly said 'thank you'. I took it back after I'd given it him. I'd meant to do that, anyway," he admitted, "but if he'd been decent about it, I'd have let him have it a bit longer."

"I bet this eb'ny's reelly pot, or somethin' painted over black," said Ginger, returning to their original discussion. "I've never heard of an eb'ny tree."

"Well, you've not heard of everythin', have you?" retorted William.

"No, but I've jolly well heard of most things," said Ginger with spirit. "I bet there's not much I've not heard of."

"Well, you'd not heard of this eb'ny, had you?"

"No, an' that's why I don't think there is such a thing. I bet you heard wrong. I bet it was em'rald or somethin' like that."

"'Course it couldn't be. Em'rald's green."

"I bet it's em'rald painted over black, then."

"I bet it isn't."

"I bet it is."

"I bet it isn't."

"I bet it is."

The argument, having reached the point at which it could apparently go on for ever, Henry intervened.

"Well, bring it," he said, "an' then we can see what it is."

"How can I?" demanded William again. "He's

mad on it. When he's not brushin' his hair with it, he's standin' an' lookin' at it with a soppy sort of smile. Seems to think no one's ever had an eb'ny hair-brush before."

"An' I bet they've not," said Ginger darkly.

"All right," said William, stung by his friends' incredulity. "I'll jolly well bring it. You wait an' see if it's anythin' painted over black. It's eb'ny, I tell you. I'll wait for a day when he's goin' out, an' I'll bring it along an' show you. Jus' fancy you never havin' heard of eb'ny!"

"Well, anyway, if there *is* such a thing," said Ginger, "an' I bet there isn't, I jolly well bet *you'd* never heard of it till your brother got this hair-brush."

William replied to this by a scornful "Huh!" and they turned to more engrossing topics, such as the possibility of navigating the pond in an old wash-tub, which Ginger had found derelict, and a clothes prop, and the purely hypothetical question of whether a bite from a cow that had been bitten by a bull that had been bitten by a horse that had been bitten by a donkey that had been bitten by a mad dog would give one hydrophobia.

The next day it turned out that Robert was going to spend the afternoon with a friend, and William decided to seize the opportunity, and take the ebony hair-brush from his bedroom, and show it to the Outlaws. The scheme worked quite well. He waited till Robert had set off for the bus, then crept quietly into his bedroom, took the ebony hair-brush from its place of honour on the dressing-table, hid it under his coat, and hurried down to the old barn. He found the

Outlaws already convinced, for Henry had made enquiries and brought full particulars.

"Eb'ny *is* a wood."

"Well, I said it was, di'n't I?" said William triumphantly.

"An' it comes from China. An' it breaks jolly easy. My aunt said she once had a walkin'-stick of it, an' it broke clean in two."

"Well, anyway, here it is," said William, bringing the brush from under his coat.

They examined it with interest.

"It's eb'ny," said Henry, assuming the air of an expert, on the strength of his aunt's walking-stick.

"Yes, it's eb'ny, all right."

"Di'n't I *tell* you it was?" said William.

"Yes, it's eb'ny," agreed the others. "S'black wood, all right."

William felt his honour to be vindicated by this general admission, and the subject of ebony—not, they felt, a particularly interesting one at the best of times—was dropped.

The hair-brush itself, however, continued to interest them. They brushed their hair with it in turn, till each assumed quite a well-groomed appearance.

"Yes, it's a jolly good one," each gave as his verdict.

"I won't bother takin' it back jus' yet," said William. "Robert won't be back till after tea. We'll put it in Ginger's bedroom to keep it safe, an' I'll take it with me when I go home."

The Outlaws were going to spend the afternoon playing in the wood and then to have tea at Ginger's. The afternoon passed satisfactorily. They tracked and retracked each other through the undergrowth.

They made a fire without attracting the keeper's attention, and cooked a mixture of cold sausage, blancmange, plum tart, and marmalade, that Ginger had succeeded in abstracting from his larder. They returned to Ginger's and ate an enormous tea, then besieged each other, in turn, in the green-house, and broke two panes of glass.

Then suddenly William remembered the hair-brush.

"Gosh!" he said. "I nearly forgot it. I'd better be takin' it back now. He was goin' to be home soon after tea."

He got the brush from Ginger's bedroom, and set off jauntily along the road. William always found a journey along a straight road rather dull, and had to introduce some diversion in order to enliven it. The diversion he introduced on this occasion was that of balancing the hair-brush on his head. It needed, of course, a certain amount of care and due regard to balance. He was delighted with his success. It only fell off once or twice. He renounced his prospective careers of burglar and detective for that of acrobat. He even managed to put on a slight swagger, and still retain the hair-brush on his head. The road led along by the river and reached the point where stepping-stones crossed the river at a shallow spot. William looked at it longingly. To cross the stepping stones balancing the hair-brush on his head would be a splendid feat. He'd be able to boast about it to the Outlaws, afterwards. And it wouldn't really be much more difficult than walking along the road.

He wouldn't go right across the river, of course. He'd just step across to the first stone to show that

WILLIAM BOWED IN RESPONSE TO THE CHEERING, AND THE
HAIR-BRUSH FELL INTO THE WATER.

he could do it. He made his way down to the river
(the brush fell off as he crossed the stile, but that, he
decided, didn't count), then stood on the bank, the
brush carefully balanced on his head. He stepped
on to the first stone without mishap. The empty
banks had vanished, and a packed and wildly-cheering
multitude had taken their place. He was a world-
famous acrobat, performing dizzy feats of daring—
feats never before performed within the memory of
man. He passed on to the second step, and stood
erect, the ebony hair-brush still secure on his head.
The cheers were redoubled. He stepped across to the
third stone. The cheering became a deafening roar.
Instinctively, he bowed slightly in response and—the
hair-brush fell into the water. Instantly, the cheering
multitudes vanished, and the world-famous acrobat
became a rather frightened small boy, who had dropped
his brother's new ebony hair-brush into the river.
The water was not deep, and it was easy enough to
recover the hair-brush and to dry the handle. But
the bristles were soaked, and no amount of rubbing
with William's already sodden handkerchief seemed
to make them any drier. The church clock struck
five. Robert might be home any minute now. That
he should find the precious hair-brush in this state
was unthinkable. And suddenly William remembered
that, in her letter, Sheila had said that the hair-brush
was "just like Daddy's". If only Daddy's could
be substituted for Robert's till Robert's was dry. . . .
But Mr. Barron was away with the rest of the family.
And then another memory occurred to him. He
remembered Robert's saying that, when he had admired
her father's ebony hair-brush, Sheila had said: "Oh,

"WHAT YOU DOING OF HERE?"
THE GARDENER SNARLED, AND
WILLIAM HASTILY WITHDREW.

he's got a much grander one in his dressing-case, but
Mummy makes him keep that for going away."

Robert had been much impressed by this evidence
of the vastness and magnificence of the Barrons'
possessions, but William, beyond thinking it all very
silly, had paid little attention to it. Now, however,
his thoughts turned to it gratefully. If Mr. Barron
used his dressing-case hair-brush when he was away,

the ebony one just like Robert's might still be on his dressing-table. If the window over the verandah hadn't had a new catch put on to it, William could open it easily with a penknife, as he used to when the house was empty. If he could put it in Robert's bedroom in the place of Robert's, till Robert's was dry, all would be well. Mr. Barron's would be duly replaced the next day, and the vengeance of an enraged Robert, which William knew by experience could be highly unpleasant, would be averted.

If the plan was to be tried (and William had already decided that it was to be tried), there was no time to be lost, so he set off at once across the fields to the Barrons' house. He entered the garden cautiously, and there met with a slight setback, for the Barrons' gardener (a bad-tempered little man whom William disliked intensely), advanced upon him threateningly.

"What you doing of here?" he snarled. "You git out or I'll half murder you."

William was accustomed to bad-tempered gardeners (as a class they seemed to run to an embittered outlook on life), but he had never before come across one with a temper quite as vicious as the Barrons' gardener. All gardeners, of course, told you that they'd half murder you if they got hold of you, but the Barrons' gardener really seemed to mean it.

William hastily withdrew, but hung about outside the gate, awaiting his opportunity. To his relief, the gardener set off almost at once from the side gate, and made his way across the fields towards the village. William entered the garden again, climbed up on to the verandah roof, and slipped back the catch of the window. The catch slid back easily and naturally, as if welcoming an old friend into his familiar haunts. He pushed up the window. The room was evidently Mr. Barron's dressing-room, and there, on a low chest of drawers, which he could reach without even putting his foot into the room, was the ebony hair-brush—exactly like the one he had dropped into the river. He resisted the temptation to explore farther, put the hair-brush into his pocket, closed the window, swarmed down the verandah pillar, and ran all the way home. Robert had not yet returned. He crept up to his bedroom, and put the hair-brush on the dressing-table. It looked a little dusty, so he took out his handkerchief and wiped it all over. As he closed the door behind him, he heard the sound of Robert's voice in the hall below and gave a gasp of relief. It had been a near thing. . . .

The next day he waited till Robert had gone out, then replaced his own hair-brush, now quite dry and presentable. The next step was to return Mr. Barron's hair-brush to The Lilacs. William was beginning to feel somewhat nervous of ebony hair-brushes. They fell into rivers on little or no provocation, and hadn't Henry's aunt's walking-stick snapped clean in two? . . . An accident with Mr. Barron's hair-brush might lead to exposure of the whole plot, and Robert's vengeance, even though he'd got his precious brush back safe and sound, would be terrible.

William took it up gingerly by the bristles, wrapped it in his handkerchief, slipped it into his pocket, made his way to The Lilacs, and replaced it without accident on Mr. Barron's dressing-table, holding it again by the bristles. And that, of course, as far as William was concerned, was the end of the incident. He had, in fact, completely forgotten it by the end of the month when the Barrons came back.

Robert went round on the evening of their return, to thank Sheila once more for her hair-brush (though he'd already written her sixteen and a half pages about it), and found the whole family in a state of great excitement.

All the silver had been stolen during their absence, and a police detective was already on the spot making enquiries. The thief had broken a pane of glass in the door that led out on to the verandah, and then put his hand in to turn the key.

"Only one clue as far as we can make out," the detective was saying. "The thief—whoever he was —left finger-prints on the hair-brush in Mr. Barron's dressing-room. They're not Mr. Barron's, anyway, or anyone else's in the house. He evidently stood at the dressing-table and brushed his hair. They're the marks of someone holding the brush pretty tightly, just as they'd hold it to brush their hair."

"But, surely it's odd that the fellow should leave finger-prints there, and nowhere else," said Mr. Barron.

"Not at all," said the detective. "That frequently happens. Just one moment's carelessness. He'd slipped off his gloves and put down his handkerchief or whatever he was using to eliminate finger-prints —saw the hair-brush and brushed his hair with it. Almost automatically, as you might say. A moment's aberration. Sometimes it's a bottle of wine. A hair-brush isn't common, of course, but it's the same idea. Just going to get ready to do the job, sees the hair-brush, and brushes his hair with it—or sees the bottle and has a drink from it—probably hardly realised that he was doing it—but there are his finger-prints and the only ones he left, and if we have any luck, those are the finger-prints that'll land the gentleman in jail."

Robert had drawn Sheila apart from the rest, and was still pouring out incoherent thanks.

"It was marvellous of you. Simply marvellous," he said. "I simply can't tell you how marvellous it was. I can't tell you what it means to me and what it will always mean to me. . . ."

But Sheila was more interested in the robbery than in Robert's hair-brush.

"Isn't it strange," she said, "that the only finger-prints were left on Daddy's hair-brush? I wonder if we shall ever catch the thief. I think we shall. The detective looks awfully clever, don't you think?"

A pang of jealousy shot through Robert's heart, and suddenly a brilliant idea occurred to him. He'd read enough detective stories to know that it is the amateur detective, never the professional one, who brings the criminal to justice. Also, on the last page, the amateur detective is invariably rewarded for his labours by the hand of the beautiful heroine, whose father he has rescued from the criminal's clutches. The stage was set, the parts assigned. Here were the hero, the heroine, the heroine's father and the professional detective. The last, Robert knew, by his perusal of detective novels, to be a man of such crass stupidity as to be utterly negligible. Robert decided to seize his rôle before anyone else appropriated it. He approached the detective, who was still holding the list of stolen silver.

"Excuse me," he said, "may I look at the list?"

The detective handed him the sheet of paper.

"Won't be any good for identification purposes," he said. "He'll probably melt it all down. . . ."

Robert read over the list in silence and handed it back to the detective. He must now start at once upon his task of bringing the criminal to justice. He didn't quite know how he was going to start on it, but he knew that he was going to start on it at once. The amateur detective wasted no time. It was only the professional detective who did that, who bungled about, ignoring clues that were just under his nose. In the last book he'd read, the hero had gone out for a ride on his motor-cycle in order to get a perspective on the affair, and had come back with an elaborate theory worked out in his head, that happened to be right in every detail, and that brought him a solution of the mystery and the heroine's hand before the end of the day. He decided to do that—to go out for a ride on his motor-cycle (fortunately, he had it with him) to get a perspective on the affair, and wait for the theory (correct in every detail) to occur suddenly to his mind. He assumed an air that was gay and easy and natural, yet at the same time stern and purposeful —the air of a man who would smile light-heartedly in the face of the most consummate danger, the air, in fact, of the amateur detective of fiction.

He was momentarily disconcerted to find that he had left a smudge of finger-marks on the paper that the detective had handed him. He'd had trouble starting up his motor-cycle, and evidently hadn't wiped his hands quite clean afterwards. But that was, after all, a mere detail compared with bringing the criminal to justice and winning the hand of the heroine.

"So sorry," he said, as he handed it back. "It's my wretched motor-bike. It oozes oil at every pore, nowadays. . . . Well, I'll be getting along."

He departed, leaving the detective staring open-mouthed at the sheet of paper that had just been put into his hand. For there, quite unmistakably, were the thief's finger-prints, the prints that had been found on the hair-brush upstairs. There was even the ziz-zag scratch on the thumb that Robert had got when experimenting with a patent tin-opener a short time ago.

* * * * *

William was sitting astride the roof of the tool-shed, surveying the prospect through an imaginary telescope, when Sheila arrived, breathless and without a hat.

"Where's Robert?" she panted.

"Dunno," said William, turning the telescope in the direction of the church spire, which he saw as a gigantic privateer bearing down on him. With a quick movement of his arm he trained his guns on it.

"Steady, my hearties," he admonished his men.

"Do come down," pleaded Sheila tearfully. "Robert's in danger, terrible danger."

That sounded rather exciting, so William abandoned his impending sea-battle for the time being, and scrambled down from the tool-shed roof.

"How's he in danger!" he demanded. "Is a lion after him, or somethin'?"

"No, no, of course not," said Sheila. "But there's been a burglary at home, and they've proved that Robert did it."

"Gosh!" said William, amazed. He thought of Robert's dull, placid, law-abiding existence. "Not *Robert*. He couldn't have."

"But he *did*. They've got proof."

"What proof've they got?" said William.

Sheila made a gesture of impatience.

"Oh, what does that matter! I haven't time to go into all that. Every minute's precious. He doesn't know that he's even suspected. We must find him and warn him quickly. We must hide him. We must get him out of the country. . . ."

Sheila was enjoying the situation, though she imagined herself to be heart-broken. Robert had risen immensely in her esteem. He wasn't, after all, the shy and awkward youth he had appeared to be. He was a daring criminal, a king, perhaps, of the underworld. His shyness and awkwardness was a blind. He controlled vast, international organisations. Criminals moved hither and thither at his bidding. He was the mysterious "chief", whom probably his underlings had never even seen, but whose every word they obeyed at peril of their lives. It was Robert who inserted those cryptic messages in the personal columns of the newspapers that were, she had always been told, directions from kings of the underworld to their subjects. Oh, how she had mis-judged him! How wrong she had been to find him dull and boring! . . . The Scarlet Pimpernel . . . Raffles. . . . It was all in the tradition, of course. And she, on her side, would be one of those cool, dauntless heroines, whom she had so often seen on the pictures, who risk their lives several times a day to save their lovers from justice. . . . But, of course,

the first thing to do was to warn him, and she couldn't do that till she knew where he was.

"*Gosh!*" William was saying. "Fancy ole Robert!" There was a new respect in his voice, too. "Has he done other ones as well?"

"Oh, I expect so," said Sheila. "I expect he's been doing it for years. They do, you know, and then they make one slip, and the police are on to them. They're on to Robert now, and we must save him."

William thought over all the burglaries in the neighbourhood that he could remember—the theft of Mrs. Bott's diamond brooch, of Mrs. Monk's fur coat, of General Moult's car. . . . And to think that Robert had done them all—that Robert, apparently intent on playing games and working for exams, in the intervals of a series of harmless flirtations, had really all the time been carrying out these daring coups. William wished he'd known. He'd liked to have had a hand in them, too. Still, as Sheila rightly pointed out, the thing to do now was to save Robert from jail. There was not, as she said, a moment to be lost. . . .

"If only we knew where he *was*," she groaned.

"I wonder how they found out," said William. "I bet that gardener told 'em."

"What gardener?"

"Your gardener. I—I—er—passed the house when you were away an' he was there an' I bet he saw Robert do it an' told them. He's a nasty sort of man."

"But he couldn't have been there while we were away," said Sheila. "Daddy had given him the sack before we went away and told him never to go near the place again. He'd been stealing vegetables and selling them."

"Well, he was there, anyway," said William.

It was at this moment that Robert returned. He was feeling rather disappointed. He had been for a ride on his motor-cycle, like the hero of the story, but no solution of the mystery had occurred to him. He left his cycle by the side door and came round to the back garden. His face lightened as his eyes fell on Sheila. She'd come to talk over the affair with him. How jolly decent of her! Together they'd thrash it out. . . .

"Oh, Robert!" she cried hysterically, as soon as she saw him. "They know . . . they know everything."

"Do they?" said Robert, slightly disappointed. "How did they find out?"

Sheila couldn't help admiring him. So calm and debonair—like all real heroes in the face of danger.

"Never mind that now," she said. "There's no time to go into all that. But they know. You must fly, Robert. Fly at once."

"Me?" said the astounded Robert. "Fly? Where? What? Why?"

"Anywhere. We'll help you. We'll try to put them off the scent till you're safely away. Now that they know you stole the silver, they . . ."

"*Me?*" interrupted Robert wildly. "*Me?* Stole the *silver?*"

They looked at him in silence. Even they could see that he wasn't acting. He hadn't stolen the silver. He wasn't a world-famous criminal. . . . Sheila was torn between relief and disappointment, and, on the whole, relief won. After all, it would have been rather a nuisance having to shield a famous criminal indefinitely. It would interfere so with one's normal activities.

"Di'n't you do it, then?" William was saying, frankly disappointed.

"'Course I didn't," snapped the flustered Robert. "Don't be such a darn little fool."

"Well then we must *prove* you didn't," said Sheila. It was, after all, almost as exciting. The wrongly-suspected lover. The brave girl, giving herself no rest till she had proved his innocence. William, too, was reconciling himself to the slightly less-alluring position. Poor old Robert—wrongly suspected! Yes, they must do their best to save him.

"Well, then, we've gotter find who did it," he said.

"B—but why should they think I did it?" gasped Robert. "I've never been near the place."

"They've found your finger-prints," said Sheila. "I'm afraid they've got a very strong case against you. Oh, don't stand there *arguing*," as Robert opened his mouth to protest. "There's no time. They may be here any minute with—with blood-hounds and things. We can talk afterwards. The thing to do now is to get you out of the country."

"But I never—never in my life . . ." stammered Robert helplessly, his eyes agog with horror, his mouth hanging open loosely. William and Sheila looked at him. Far indeed, was the cool, daring, master criminal of their imagination. But his horror and dismay roused their protective instinct.

"We'll stand by you to the end, Robert," Sheila assured him stoutly.

"B—b—but, I say, you *do* believe I didn't, don't you?" pleaded Robert.

F

WILLIAM OPENED THE DOOR. "IT'S A GOOD PLACE FOR
YOU TO HIDE," HE SAID GLEEFULLY.

"Of course I do."

"Well, look here," said William, "if Robert didn't,
someone else did. And—I say—that gardener man
might have seen someone hanging about. He was

THE UNHAPPY ROBERT, STILL PROTESTING, WAS PUSHED
INTO THE COAL SHED.

there the day I—er—came along. He might've
noticed someone sort of hanging about."

"Why, yes," said Sheila, relieved by this definite
suggestion. It sounded grand and resourceful to

talk about getting Robert "out of the country", but she hadn't the faintest idea how to set about it. "Yes, that's what we'll do. We'll hide Robert here and we'll go to the gardener's cottage—I know where he lives—and ask him if he saw anyone hanging about. Where shall we hide Robert?" She glanced round the garden and noticed the coal-shed just beyond the tool-shed that had been William's galleon. There was a key in the lock. "Let's hide him there, and lock him in. They won't think of looking there, and, even if they do, it will take them some time to break open the door. You'll keep well under the coal, won't you, Robert? So that if they look through the window they won't see you."

The unhappy Robert, still protesting, was pushed into the coal-shed and the key turned on him.

"Here!" he shouted through the door. "Here! Wait a minute. I don't understand. Why should they think *I* did it? I never . . ."

But Sheila and William were already out of earshot, running quickly up the road in the direction of the gardener's cottage. At the end of the road could be seen the figures of a policeman and Mr. Barron. They were evidently coming to interview Robert.

"Oh, dear!" gasped Sheila. "I do hope he keeps well underneath the coal. At any rate, they evidently haven't brought any bloodhounds. . . ."

When they were near the cottage, they slackened pace.

"We'll have to be very careful," said Sheila. "He's an awful-tempered man. . . ."

"I know," said William.

"He had an awful row with Daddy, when Daddy

gave him the sack. We'll have to be very tactful or he won't tell us anything. I haven't even any money to tip him with, have you?"

"No," said William.

"Well. . . . Let's knock, anyway."

They went up to the little green door, and knocked. There was no answer. They knocked again. Still there was no answer.

"Bother!" said Sheila. "He's out."

"I thought I saw him in the kitchen," said William.

"You couldn't have. . . . Oh, dear, what shall we do now? I suppose we must go back to Robert and try to get him out of the country. . . ."

They walked back disconsolately down the road. Then William said: "I'm *sure* I saw him in the kitchen jus' before we knocked."

"You couldn't have," said Sheila again. "Oh, dear, what *shall* we do about Robert? I don't know how people get people out of the country, do you?"

"No. . . . Let's go back an' try once more."

They returned to the cottage.

"He must have been in, "said William. "The curtains are drawn now, an' they weren't drawn when we were there before. Let's see what he's doin'."

"We can't with the curtains drawn."

"There's a little chink at the top. If I climb that tree I bet I can see all right."

He climbed the tree quickly and silently. Through the chink at the top of the curtains he could see the gardener quite plainly. He had taken up several boards in the floor of his kitchen and made some sort of excavation beneath, and into this cavity he was

carefully transferring from a sack the silver that had
been stolen from Mr. Barron.

*   *   *   *   *

The tumult and shouting had died. The silver had
been recovered. The gardener was safely under
lock and key. Robert, rescued from the coal-shed,
was hoarsely, from beneath a thick film of coal dust,
demanding explanations of everybody around him.
William, who had discovered the real culprit and
fetched the police to the spot, was preening himself
as the hero of the occasion. It had been *his* idea to go
to the gardener's cottage. It had been *his* idea to
climb the tree. . . . Robert ought to be jolly grateful
to him. Mr. Barron ought to be jolly grateful to him.
The police ought to be jolly grateful to him. Everyone
ought to be jolly grateful to him. . . . Scotland
Yard ought to give him a medal or something. . . .

"But why should you have suspected *me?*" Robert
was demanding wildly.

"Well, sir," said the detective, "we found your
finger-prints—they were quite plain—on Mr. Barron's
hair-brush."

"On Mr. Barron's hair-brush!" echoed Robert
faintly. "But I've never been near it."

William had collapsed like a pricked balloon. For
the first time, he remembered the incident of the ebony
hair-brush, remembered how carefully and gingerly
he had carried it back by its bristles, realised that the
finger-prints where Robert had innocently held it to
brush his hair would still be there on its virgin surface,
understood how the whole horrible misunderstanding
had happened. . . . He looked fearfully at Robert.
Robert was not, after all, a daredevil criminal, a lord

of the underworld, but he could be terrible enough for all that. His covering of coal dust made him look more formidable than usual. The whites of his eyes stood out horribly.

William decided not to draw attention to his own part in the capture of the thief. He decided, instead, to fade from the scene as quietly and unobtrusively as possible. Sooner or later, he knew, the story of the ebony hair-brush would be dragged from him and then he would have to face that dreadful coal-coloured figure of vengeance. . . . But better later than sooner. It was long after his bedtime, and he thought the best thing to do was to go to bed. That would put off explanations till to-morrow. William always believed in putting off explanations till to-morrow. He murmured inaudible farewells, and withdrew very quietly from the circle.

"I've no doubt that there's some simple explanation of it, my boy," said Mr. Barron mildly, "but the fact remains that your finger-prints were found on my hair-brush."

Robert looked round the group, and noticed the figure of William quietly sloping off. It was eloquent in every line of a guilty desire to escape notice. And, suddenly, he remembered that when he came back from spending the afternoon with a friend a week or so ago, he had seen William on the landing, and had had a strong suspicion that he had just come out of his bedroom. He had hurried anxiously in, but found everything untouched—his precious ebony hair-brush quite safe. But had everything been untouched? He remembered thinking that the ebony hair-brush wasn't just where it had been when he'd left it. . . . The ebony hair-brush. . . . That was evidently the key to the whole mystery, and, as usual, William was at the bottom of it. He sprang forward, clutched William by the collar, and dragged him back. "Now," he said grimly, "you tell us all you know about this."

William, after a few experimental wriggles, surrendered to the inevitable with as good a grace as possible. It would have to be sooner, after all. He looked at the circle of tense and interested faces round him, and his spirits rose somewhat. He was the centre of the stage, and William always enjoyed being the centre of the stage. And, anyway, he could postpone Robert's vengeance by spinning the tale out indefinitely. He was an expert at doing that. He assumed a bland and innocent expression.

"Well," he began, "it wasn't really my fault, but the way it happened was this. . . ."

CHAPTER VII

AUNT LOUIE'S BIRTHDAY PRESENT

THE Outlaws had called at the Brown's house for William. A half-holiday lay before them, every minute of it precious.

They stood at the side door, discussing the best method of spending it.

"Let's go'n' try 'n' dam the stream by the ole barn," said William. "I bet we could make a fine lake there. . . . Right over the field."

"All right," they agreed. "Come on!"

It was at this moment that Mrs. Brown called: "William, dear," from upstairs.

Mrs. Brown was in bed with a headache—one of the devastating headaches that occasionally, very occasionally, laid her low. William mounted the stairs, assuming the expression of stern gloom that he considered suitable for a sick-room.

He opened the door and tiptoed elaborately to the bedside, where Mrs. Brown lay with closed eyes.

"Yes, mother," he said in a sepulchral whisper.

"I want you to do something for me, dear," said Mrs. Brown. "I've suddenly remembered that it's the last day for the South African mail, and I haven't got Aunt Louie's birthday present yet. I forgot all about it till this moment. I wondered if you'd go down to Hadley and get it for me, dear, then I can post it this evening. Will you?"

Aunt Louie was an old school friend of Mrs. Brown's. She had been over to England a few years ago, and William remembered her well. She was fat and jolly and very understanding about Red Indians and smugglers and pirates. She'd been into the woods with him, and helped him cook a mixture of sausages and sardines and bacon rinds over a fire. William felt that, if he had to give up his precious half-holiday, he'd rather give it up to Aunt Louie than to anyone else.

"Yes," he said, in his sibilant sick-room whisper.

"She's coming over to England again next year," went on Mrs. Brown. "And I shouldn't like her to think I'd forgotten her. . . . Now, listen very carefully, dear. I want you to get a tea-cloth that I saw in Hemmett's in Hadley last week. It's linen with filet lace let in, and it's ten and six. If it's sold, any of Hemmett's white tea-cloths at ten and six would do. They're all very pretty. About thirty-six inches square. Can you remember all that, dear?"

"Yes," hissed William gloomily.

It was going to be a pretty mess-up of a half-holiday, he thought, going into Hadley for a tea-cloth instead of damming the stream and making a lake. . . .

But William, despite his many faults, had a kind heart, and it always distressed him to see his usually bustling, busy mother laid low.

"My purse is on the dressing-table," said Mrs. Brown. "Take out a ten-shilling note and a sixpence. If you bring it all back all right I'll give you sixpence for yourself."

William felt slightly consoled by this promise.

"Thanks," he hissed. Then he looked at her

solicitously. "Would you like me to bring you
somethin' from Hadley, mother?"

"No, thank you, dear."

"Not a nice cream bun?"

A flicker of agony passed over Mrs. Brown's features.

"No, thank you, dear."

"Some sherbet?"

"No, thank you," said Mrs. Brown, faintly. "Get
the money now, dear, and go as quietly as you can."

William tiptoed across to the dressing-table, but his
tiptoeing was always of a somewhat elephantine
nature. He banged into a chair, and knocked over a
bottle of hair lotion on the dressing-table, before he
finally found the purse. He took a ten-shilling note
and a sixpence, put them carefully into his pocket,
and made his way, still tiptoeing, to the door.

"Don't bang it, dear," pleaded Mrs. Brown faintly.

William gave his whole attention to not banging
the door. He closed it by infinitesimal inches, and
took so long that his mother's nerves were strained
to breaking-point before it finally reached its objective.
The effect was somewhat marred by his immediately
slipping on the top step and falling all the way downstairs. His voice, raised in angry self-justification to
the housemaid, who came out of the kitchen to ask
him indignantly what he was making all that clatter
for with his mother ill in bed, assured Mrs. Brown that
he had sustained no vital injury, and she relaxed on
her pillows again, trying to calm her jangled nerves.

Meantime, William made sure that the ten-shilling
note and the sixpence were safe, then rejoined the
Outlaws at the side door.

"I say, I've gotter go down to Hadley," he said

gloomily.   "I've gotter go 'n' buy a rotten ole
birthday present for an ole aunt."

Their faces fell, but they rallied quickly to his support.

"We'll all come," they said.   "We can go 'n' dam
the stream afterwards.   We'll all come an' help you
choose it."

"I've not even gotter choose it," said William, still
more gloomily.   "I've gotter get a rotten ole tea-
cloth she saw at Hemmett's."

"A tea-cloth!" they echoed in disgust.

"Well, of course, they *like* things like that," said
Ginger philosophically.

"I dunno," said William doubtfully.   "She seemed
sort of different."

They walked down to Hadley, discussing Aunt
Louie.   They all remembered her.

"She was jolly good at makin' fires," said Ginger.

"Yes, an' she took us all into Hadley four times
to give us ice-creams."

"An' she could make that noise they do in Switzer-
land."

"Yodel," put in Henry, with a superior air.

"Well, I said that, din' I?" said William.   "*You*
can't do it, anyway."

"I never said I could.   Neither can you."

"I nearly can."

"Well, so can I, nearly."

"I bet you can't.   Go on, do it."

"Do it yourself."

For a few moments nerve-shattering cat-calls
rent the air, as all the Outlaws took part in the com-
petition.   Then they settled down again to a discussion of Aunt Louie.

"NOW, THAT PISTOL'D BE JOLLY USEFUL TO HER," SAID
DOUGLAS.

"She took us out to tea, an' gave us orange squash,
an' cream buns, an' let us go on an' on an' on. . . ."

"An' she gave us each half a crown when she went
back."

"A *tea*-cloth!" ejaculated Ginger in disgust.

"I bet she doesn't want one really," said William. "I bet she'd rather have somethin' int'restin'. It's jus' that my mother can't think of anythin' but tea-cloths an' such like. *She* likes tea-cloths, an' thinks everyone else must, too. Grown-ups are like that. They think that if *they* like dull things, so mus' every-one else. That's why they give us such rotten presents at Christmas."

"I don't see what she'd *do* with a tea-cloth in South Africa," said Douglas thoughtfully. "I once saw a film of it, an' it was all wild country an' lions an' little huts an' savidges. I didn't see any tea-cloths or anythin' like that. The only meals they had, what *I* could see, were under trees an' on rocks, tryin' to get out of the way of lions an' savidges. I bet she won't know what a tea-cloth is."

"She saw 'em when she was in England," Henry reminded them.

"Yes, but that was a long time ago. I bet she's forgotten by now."

"Pity not to send her somethin' reely useful . . ." murmured Ginger.

They had reached Hadley now, and stood looking into the window of a toy-shop that always attracted them.

"Now, that pistol'd be jolly useful to her," said Douglas. "I bet you want no end of pistols in a country like South Africa, with all those lions an' savidges."

"It's not a real one," Henry reminded him.

"I know, but it'd sort of give 'em a scare. She could use it to scare 'em with when she'd run out of bullets for her real one, or when the real one was bein' mended or somethin'. They wouldn't know it wasn't a real one, an' I bet it'd scare 'em right enough. If I was out there, with all those lions an' savidges an' things, I bet I'd be jolly glad to have it."

"Well, let's get it, then," said Ginger in a business-like manner. "It's only two an' six. It'll leave quite a lot for a tea-cloth. An', anyway, she doesn't want a tea-cloth."

William hesitated for a moment, but Ginger's contention seemed fair enough, so they all trooped into the toy shop.

The pistol was examined, approved and purchased.

"I bet she'll be jolly grateful for it," said Douglas. "I shun't be surprised if it saves her life. You know, a savidge might be just comin' at her with a spear, same as they did in that picture, an' she'd lost her real pistol, an' pointed this at him, an' he'd think it was a real one an' run off."

William, who felt that he'd already saved Aunt Louie's life several times, looked complacent and important.

A magnificent drum had caught Henry's attention. He took it up and examined it.

"This is a jolly fine one," he said. "I bet this'd be jolly useful, too. She could beat on it to call the other white people to help her when the savidges were attacking her. I think drums are jolly useful in savidge countries. You can send messages in code on 'em. She could beat so many beats to mean 'lion', an' so many beats to mean 'savidges'. Why, they could make up a sort of langwidge on drums. Each letter so many beats. She could send out messages, even if her hut was all s'rounded by lions an' savidges. I bet we ought to get her the drum. It's only two an' six, too."

The Outlaws eagerly purchased the drum. By this time the tea-cloth had been completely forgotten. They walked down the street, discussing their purchases.

The next shop they stopped at was also a toy-shop, a less magnificent one than the first, but still a favourite with the Outlaws. Reposing on a shelf, among a selection of small boats and engines and miscellaneous articles, beneath the notice, "All these 6d. each", was a compass.

"*Look!*" said Ginger excitedly. "That would be fine for her. She'd be able to find her way with it when she was lost in the bush."

"It's the veldt in South Africa," said Henry.

"Well, whatever it is," said Ginger impatiently, "an' I bet it's the bush, too. Anyway she'd be able to find her way in it when she was lost. I bet it'd be jolly useful."

The Outlaws went into the shop and purchased the compass. Then they looked round the shop. It was Douglas who found the box of fireworks left over from the Fifth of November, marked down to two shillings.

"I say!" he said. "This'd be jolly useful. She could use 'em to tame the savidges. They'd think it was magic, an' they'd be scared, an' prob'ly end by makin' her queen. I once read a story where that happened. I bet that'd be jolly useful."

The fireworks seemed almost a necessity, so the Outlaws bought them and then went on to the next shop. The next shop was another of their favourites.

It was an attractive medley of seeds, bulbs, gardening sundries, birds, goldfish, and tortoises.

The Outlaws flattened their noses, as usual, against the window.

"I 'spect there's lots of coloured birds and goldfish out there," said William at last, "but I bet there aren't any tortoises. An' I bet one'd be nice company for her. I don't expect she can have dogs or cats, 'cause the lions'd get 'em, but she could keep a tortoise in the hut with her, an' it'd be jolly good comp'ny. We had one once an' it would have got to know me all right, but Jumble would never let it put its head out so we had to give it away. But I bet it'd be jolly useful in South Africa. She could throw it at a lion if it was springin' at her. Or she could show it to the savidges to help tame 'em. I bet they've never seen one before. They'd think it was a sort of magic, too."

All these statements seemed irrefutable to the Outlaws, and they felt it incumbent upon them to buy the tortoise at once.

They selected a large, handsome, half-crown one. As Ginger said:

"We'd better get her a really good one. It might jus' help to make the natives choose her queen. She might train it to carry messages for her, too, same as a pigeon does. They're a bit slow, but that's all the better, 'cause the savidges mightn't notice it was movin' at all. They'd jus' think it was a bit of rock, an' all the time it would be fetchin' help for her when her hut was s'rounded by savidges."

The Outlaws contemplated this picture with deep gratification.

"Of course, she'd have to train it a bit," added

William, "but I bet they're easy enough to train. I bet I could've trained ours if Jumble'd ever let him put his head out. I'd like to have another myself, some time. I bet I could train Jumble to like it. I'd put bits of butterscotch on it. Jumble likes butterscotch."

Laden with their parcels, they set off joyously homewards.

"I bet she'll be jolly grateful," said Ginger.

"I bet we've saved her life lots of times," said Douglas.

"P'raps she'll send us a lion cub back," said Henry. "I've always wanted a lion cub. I asked for one my last birthday, but no one gave me one."

William, however, was growing rather silent. He had suddenly remembered the tea-cloth. He had no doubt at all of Aunt Louie's gratitude, but he was less sure of his mother's.

At the gate he looked apprehensively towards the house.

"I think you'd better go now," he said to the others. "I've gotter 'splain to my mother about these presents an' she might not understand. Not jus' at first, anyway. I won't take 'em straight into the house. I'll leave 'em at the gate, where she can't see 'em, then, when I've 'splained, I'll come out an' fetch 'em in an' show 'em her. She's never been in South Africa, you see, so she may not understand quite at first. I'll have to 'splain. . . ."

He put the parcels by the gate, carefully arranging them so that they could not be seen from the windows, shut the tortoise in the summer-house, out of Jumble's way, took his leave absently of the Outlaws, then walked slowly and with a slightly sinking heart towards the house. He was realising that the explanations were going to be more difficult than they had appeared to be in the glamorous atmosphere of the toy and tortoise shops. There, in fact, they had seemed simple and obvious. He had forgotten, for the time being, the colossal unreasonableness of the grown-up world. . . . He was a kindly boy at heart, and he loved his mother, but he couldn't resist a sneaking hope that her headache would now be so bad that she would have forgotten tea-cloths, and Aunt Louie, and mails, and South Africa and everything else. . . .

The hope, however, proved fruitless. His mother was better, so much better that she had dressed and come downstairs, and was quite looking forward to her tea. "Well, dear," she said brightly to William, "did you get Aunt Louie's present?"

"Yes, I got Aunt Louie's present, all right," said William non-committally.

"I'm so glad," said Mrs. Brown. "I was so afraid that they might have sold it. Where have you put it, dear? We'll post it after tea."

"Well . . ." began William slowly, wondering how on earth he was going to break the news, and wondering also, for the first time, how on earth they were going to despatch the tortoise to South Africa.

But, at this moment, fate provided a diversion, and the diversion was the arrival of Aunt Louie herself. A car drew up at the gate, and Aunt Louie rushed in with a flurry of greeting and explanation. She'd decided to come over for her visit to England this year, instead of next. She'd decided quite suddenly, so that there hadn't been time to let anyone know. She was just descending on people, she said. . . . She was going, now, to stay with an old aunt who lived in the neighbourhood, and she had called to see Mrs. Brown on the way. William watched and listened with increasing gloom. She was a superior specimen of grown-up, of course, but she was a grown-up, nevertheless, hemmed in by the mysterious conventions and taboos that govern the grown-up world. He suddenly felt less sure of her reception of her presents. Moreover, she lived in a part of South Africa called Cape Town, and it became clear from her conversation that the presents would be less useful in that part of Africa than had appeared when the Outlaws were choosing them.

"Do you know," said Mrs. Brown suddenly, "I was just going to post your birthday present. William had fetched it for me this afternoon because I had a headache. I do hope you'll like it. Bring it here to Aunt Louie, will you, William dear?"

"Well . . ." began William again, searching desperately for words to explain the situation, when fate provided another diversion. This time it was Mrs. Monks, the vicar's wife. She greeted Mrs. Brown and Aunt Louie, then turned, beaming, to William.

"You've won the badge, dear boy," she said.

William gaped at her.

"The badge?" he said.

"Yes, dear," said Mrs. Monks. "The badge for the best contribution to the Poor Kiddies' Summer Treat." William still gaped at her, and she turned to Aunt Louie. "You see," she went on brightly, "I'd asked all those dear boys and girls to give me prizes for my Poor Kiddies' Summer Treat, and I'd promised to give a badge to the one who sent the best contribution. I said that I was coming round this afternoon to collect them, but I found that this dear boy had thoughtfully left his contribution just at the gate, to save me the trouble of coming up to the house. A beautiful drum and toy pistol—though I don't really approve of weapons of war, even as toys—and a compass, and a box of fireworks. By far the best contribution I've had, dear boy, and immensely to your credit. I'm afraid you must have emptied your money-box, but I'm sure that the Poor Kiddies' delight will amply repay you. I've given your things the very best position on the platform, and if you like to come round to the Village Hall any time this afternoon to see them, I'm sure you'll feel proud. These little deeds of self-sacrifice and kindness to others, dear boy, bring their own reward, as, no doubt, you've already discovered. . . . And here is the badge."

She bent down and pinned a brooch on to William's coat. It was composed of an indecipherable wool motif, stitched on to a safety-pin, and was the proud work of Mrs. Monks's own hand. She was a great believer in badges. . . .

William stared glassily in front of him. He couldn't think of anything to say or do. The situation had got completely beyond him. . . . He vaguely remembered Mrs. Monks asking him for a contribution of toys for prizes for the Poor Kiddies' Summer Treat, but he'd never given the matter another thought. And he realised, too late, that he'd been so anxious to hide his purchases from sight of the windows that he'd left them fully exposed to the road.

"But, William," said Mrs. Brown, bewildered, "I

didn't know you'd bought anything for a Summer
Treat. . . ."

Mrs. Monks smiled brightly, patted William's head,
and tucked a straying end of the wool motif behind
the safety-pin.

"Ah, that is as it should be, isn't it?" she said.
"One's left hand should never know what one's right
hand does. In my eyes, at any rate, it always detracts
from the value of any good deed when it's trumpeted
abroad. I'm so glad that this dear boy didn't trumpet
his. . . ."

She was thinking, once again, that she must have
misjudged William, and that he couldn't really be
such a dreadful boy as he'd always seemed. She tried
to make up for the injustice she'd done him in her
thoughts by turning on to him the full force of her
most effusive manner. She patted his head again.
"The Poor Kiddies will be delighted, dear boy. "*Dear*
boy. *Delighted*." She threw an anxious glance at
the badge. "If it comes off the pin, dear, just bring
it round to me and I'll put another stitch into it. . . .
And now, I must run back to the Poor Kiddies."

When she had gone, Mrs. Brown looked at William
in increasing bewilderment.

"Surely, dear," she said at last, "one toy would
have been enough."

"Well, I—er—I sort of thought p'raps they'd like
more," said William desperately.

"I didn't know you'd got enough money for all
those."

"Er—yes, I—I sort of had," said William, speaking
in a hoarse voice and gazing straight in front of him.

The dénouement was bound to bring retribution

in its train, and his one idea now was to postpone the dénouement as long as possible.

But Aunt Louie was not interested in Mrs. Monks or the Poor Kiddies or William's contribution to the Summer Treat. She was talking about the aunt with whom she was going to stay

"And a perfectly dreadful thing's happened, my dear," she was saying to William's mother. "The very last time she wrote, she asked me to bring her over one of those wooden figures the natives make, when I came home. You know, very roughly carved, and a few details put in with poker-work—animals and savages. They sell them to tourists. She'd taken a fancy to one she'd seen and set her heart on one. And I completely forgot all about it till I was driving along in the car a few minutes ago. I shall never live it down. She takes offence at nothing at all. And she's my only rich aunt. . . . I can't even pretend that I didn't get her letter, because I answered it. She'll never forgive me as long as she lives. She'll probably cut me out of her will altogether. She's capable of it. It's the only thing she's ever asked me to do for her and, of course, she'll think I shouldn't have had any other idea but the wretched thing in my mind from the moment I got her letter. . . ."

"That reminds me," said Mrs. Brown. "I was just going to give you your present when Mrs. Monks came in, wasn't I? Run and get it, will you, William, dear?"

There was a hunted look on William's face. He made another desperate attempt to postpone the dénouement.

"I'll take you to it," he said to Aunt Louie.

Mrs. Brown looked surprised. Why ever couldn't
the child bring the tea-cloth here to Louie, instead of
taking Louie to the tea-cloth? Still, she was a little
glad of the respite. Her headache was threatening
again, and Louie was just a trifle tiring.

"Very well," she murmured.

Mystified, Aunt Louie followed William to the

"IT'S YOUR PRESENT," SAID WILLIAM.

"HOW VERY SWEET OF YOUR MOTHER," SAID AUNT LOUIE
FAINTLY. "DO YOU KNOW, I'VE NEVER HAD A TORTOISE
IN MY LIFE BEFORE."

summer-house. He opened the door and stood aside. She peered about her, still more mystified. Then her bewildered gaze fell upon a tortoise that was making a slow, experimental journey across the floor.

"Whatever's that?" she said.

"A tortoise," said William.

"Yes, I know it's a tortoise. I mean. . . ."

"It's your present," said William.

"*What?*"

"Your present," repeated William stonily.

"Your mother's birthday present?"

"Yes."

"To *me*?"

"Yes."

For a moment Aunt Louie seemed too bewildered for words—then she rallied her forces.

"How sweet of her!" she said faintly. "How very sweet of her!" She considered the question in silence for another few moments. "Do you know, I've never had a tortoise in my life before."

"She—she thought p'raps you hadn't," said William. "They're jolly good pets."

"I'm sure they are. Er—what made your mother think of it?" she added wonderingly.

William pretended not to hear this and led her back to the drawing-room.

"How sweet of you, dear!" she said to Mrs. Brown. "Thank you so much."

Mrs. Brown had looked slightly surprised to see Aunt Louie come into the room empty-handed.

"Has William given it you?"

"Yes. . . . I think it's sweet."

"I thought it rather pretty, myself," said Mrs. Brown. "So dainty."

"Er—yes," agreed Aunt Louie doubtfully, thinking that dainty was not precisely the word she would have chosen herself.

"You haven't got it with you?" said Mrs. Brown.

"No, I left it where it was. It seemed quite happy there. But, my dear, how *would* you have sent it out to South Africa if I hadn't happened to come back like this?"

"By parcel post," said Mrs. Brown, looking mildly surprised.

"Parcel post!" laughed Aunt Louie. "My dear, it would have got squashed."

"You could have ironed it out," said Mrs. Brown.

Aunt Louie laughed again, thinking that Mrs. Brown was joking. Mrs. Brown looked at her in increasing perplexity.

"Do you know, I haven't the faintest idea what to feed it on," went on Aunt Louie.

Mrs. Brown put her hand to her head. Was she mad, or was Louie?

"What, exactly, *have* I given you for a birthday present?" she cried.

"A tortoise," answered Aunt Louie.

"A—*what?*" screamed Mrs. Brown.

"A tortoise," answered Aunt Louie calmly.

Mrs. Brown looked around and her gaze fell on William, who sat between them, staring in front of him with his glassy stare, his freckled face blank and expressionless. She knew she need look no further.

"*William!*" she said sternly. "What's the meaning of this?"

William drew a deep breath. "Well, you see," he began, "it was like this. . . ."

"What did you do with the ten and six I gave you?" put in Mrs. Brown hastily, knowing that if William were not tied down to hard facts he would go on talking for ever.

"I spent it on presents for her," said William. "I did, honest. I bought her that drum an' pistol an' things."

"That *what?*" said Mrs. Brown wildly.

"Drum an' pistol an' things," said William patiently.

"But—but I told you to get a tea-cloth," said Mrs. Brown.

"I know, but I didn't think she'd want a tea-cloth. I thought she'd want these things. You see, I'd got a sort of idea that South Africa was a *wilder* sort of place than what it axshully seems to be, an' we thought those things'd come in useful, 'cause . . ."

"But William, that's no excuse at all," said Mrs. Brown. Her face was stern and angry and William realised resignedly that the process of retribution had begun.

"It's inexcusable. I shall tell your father the minute he——"

Then fate provided yet another diversion, for Mrs. Monks re-entered the room.

"I've just popped in from the Village Hall," she said. "The Poor Kiddies have all had their prizes, and yours," she beamed at William, "were *quite* the most popular. There was one that none of them wanted at all, and, really, I don't wonder. It's such a very clumsy, badly-made thing, and I'm really surprised

at anyone sending it, but I thought that our little
badge-holder had a right to anything left over, so
I've brought it along just in case. . . . It might
do for you to give to some young relative or . . ."
She burrowed in her bag and brought out a roughly-
carved, wooden giraffe, with spots and eyes of poker-
work. She put it in William's hand. "Do what you
like with it, dear boy. I believe it came from South
Africa, but it's really very badly made. Our dear,
English workmen do far better work. I'm sorry
there's not something better left over, but I'm sure
that you really don't want any reward for your good
deed. And now I must run back to the Poor Kiddies.
They're just going to play Nuts in May." She threw
another anxious glance at the badge. "I think you'd
better bring it round to the Vicarage for another
stitch in the morning, dear. It looks a little insecure.
Forgive me rushing in and out like this, Mrs. Brown.
I haven't another second. Good-bye. . . ."

Aunt Louie was staring at the uncouth wooden
creature with the eyes of a drowning man who sees a
rope flung to him.

"It's one of them," she burst out, as soon as the
door was closed on Mrs. Monks. "It's what she asked
me to bring from Africa. Oh, William, do let me have
it. It's worth untold gold to me."

William handed it to her.

"I don't want it," he said.

She took it and clasped it to her breast.

"Oh, thank you, William," she said. "I can never
thank you enough." She turned to Mrs. Brown.
"Let it be my birthday present," she said. "I'd
rather have it than a hundred million tea-cloths. And

don't be cross with William," she pleaded. "He's saved my life. Promise you won't."

Mrs. Brown sighed.

"All right," she said, "but he's really very naughty."

"He's not," said Aunt Louie. "If he'd bought the tea-cloth, I'd be completely done for."

"Very well," said Mrs. Brown. Her headache had come on again, and she didn't really care about anything but getting back to bed.

"And I must fly, now," said Aunt Louie. She waved the giraffe exultantly.

"I can never thank you enough, William, dear."

She departed in her car, still waving the wooden giraffe out of the window.

"It was really very naughty of you, William," said Mrs. Brown feebly, "but in the circumstances . . ."

She went upstairs, took two aspirins, and retired to bed again.

William carefully unpinned his badge, carried it across the room at arm's length, as though it were some noxious insect, and dropped it into the fire. Then he drew a deep breath. Well, he thought, after all that fuss about nothing, he could at last go and collect the other Outlaws and start damming the stream. He'd taken a lot of trouble choosing a nice present for Aunt Louie, and he hadn't got anything out of it.

Then he brightened as he suddenly remembered something. He'd got the tortoise. . . .

CHAPTER VIII

WILLIAM AND THE DENTIST

"I 'VE made an appointment for you with the dentist this afternoon, William," said Mrs. Brown, "and Ethel's very kindly going to take you there."

William gazed at her in stricken silence for a moment, then: "*Me?*" he said faintly. "The *dentist?* I've not got toothache nor nothin'."

Mrs. Brown sighed. They had the same argument every time.

"No, dear, but it's most important to have your teeth examined twice a year. You always do, you know. It's over six months since you went last time."

William shuddered at the memory.

"Yes," he said, "an' there was nothin' wrong with my teeth then. I'd not got toothache nor nothin', an' he nearly torchered me to death. I can still feel it if I think about it long enough."

"Then there must have been something wrong, dear."

"No, there wasn't," persisted William hotly. "That's jus' the point. If I'd gotter go to him 'cause I'd got toothache, there'd be some sense in it. I'd put up with bein' torchered then. But my teeth are abs'lutely all right. Well, look at 'em." He barred his gums ferociously. "An' yet I've gotter go an' be torchered same as people in history, jus' for nothin'."

"Don't be silly, William," said Mrs. Brown. "There must have been something wrong or he wouldn't have done anything."

"Wouldn't he?" said William darkly. "They're my teeth, aren't they? Not his. I know all right when there's anythin' wrong with 'em. An' there never *is* anythin' wrong with them. He's one of those people what ought to be in prison for torcherin' people. This Prevention of Cruelty to Children thing goes on messin' about with bazaars an' such like, an' lets dentists torcher children without even tryin' to stop 'em. I wrote to 'em after the last time, but they never answered." Seeing that his mother remained unmoved by this aspect of the case, he hastily switched over to another. "It's really my teeth I'm thinkin' of . . ." he said. "I don't mind a bit of pain, but if he goes on, time after time, messin' 'em about an' diggin' at 'em when they're quite all right, I won't have any left by the time I'm grown up, an' then I'll have to starve to death. It's not good for 'em to keep disturbin' the roots. They're same as plants that way. They die off if you keep on an' on at 'em, disturbin' the roots. Mine are all right if they're left alone. Some teeth *are* all right if they're left alone, an' mine are that kind. Well, look at pots an'—an' milk jugs an' things like that. You don't take *them* to be mended before they're broke, do you? It's same as takin' boots and shoes to be mended before they're wore out. Just a waste of money. I want to *keep* my teeth. I don't want their roots disturbed on an' on an' on, till they've all died off an' I can't eat nor talk nor anythin'. . . ."

But it was obvious that his mother was no longer

"WILD ANIMALS DON'T GO TO DENTISTS," SAID WILLIAM.

G

listening to him. She had gone to her desk and was adding up tradesmen's books. She had had, perforce, to acquire the art of shutting William's voice out of her consciousness, just as some people have to acquire the art of ignoring the wireless. Otherwise she would never have got anything done. She finished the books and went into the kitchen to speak to Cook. William followed her.

"Wild animals don't go to dentists," he said.

"What, dear? said Mrs. Brown, breaking off the conversation with Cook. "No, of course, wild animals don't go to dentists. Don't say such silly things."

"I jolly well wish I was one. Anyway, my teeth are jus' as good as a wild animal's, so why should I have 'em ruined by dentists if wild animals don't?" Another thought occurred to him. "I jolly well wish they *did* have to go to dentists. I'd like *him* to have to do a lion's teeth. I bet it wouldn't put up with it same as I have to. I bet it'd start springin' at him the minute he got his drill thing down, an' I wouldn't do anythin' to help him, even if I was there." He warmed to his theme. "I think that every dentist ought to have to do a wild animal's teeth by lor, jus' to punish them for torcherin' people. I bet there wouldn't be many of 'em left after that, an' I jolly well wouldn't be sorry. I don't know why anyone ever started 'em at all. I bet that, when ordin'ry torcherin' in the Tower an' such like was stopped by lor, the torcherers set up as dentists, an' I bet all those little pickaxes an' things they use are what was left of the torcher instruments out of the torcher chambers." Still talking, he followed his mother back to the dining-

room. "First thing I'd do if I was made Prime
Minister, would be to stop dentists by lor. People's
teeth'd be all right if it wasn't for dentists messin'
'em about an' disturbin' the roots an' such like. I
bet that, if once dentists were put a stop to by lor,
there'd never be anythin' wrong with people's teeth
ever again."

Mrs. Brown, who had taken her work-basket and
sat down by the fire, looked at him as if surprised to
find him still there.

"Hadn't you better go out, dear?" she suggested.
"It's such a nice morning."

"Huh!" said William bitterly. "It's a nice
mornin' for people what aren't bein' torchered to
death."

"Well, dear," Mrs. Brown reminded him mildly,
as she hunted for her favourite darning-needle, "you
aren't being tortured to death."

"No, but you want me to be," said William. "Your
own son, an' you're sendin' me off to the torcherers."

"He may find nothing to be done," said Mrs. Brown,
as she broke off a length of darning wool and threaded
her needle.

"*Him?*" said William with biting sarcasm. "*Him*
find nothin' to be done? What's he there for with all
his little pickaxes and things? Torcherers can always
find somethin' to be done."

"William, dear, do go out and play at something,"
said Mrs. Brown patiently. "I'm so tired of hearing
you talk."

"An' what about *me?*" demanded William. "If
listenin' to someone *talkin'* about bein' torchered was
all I gotter do, I wouldn't mind. It's bein' *torchered*

I'm tired of." He went into the hall and came back, struck by a sudden idea. "Savages don't have 'em," he said.

"Have what, dear?" said Mrs. Brown, tearing her mind away from a consideration of the next day's menus.

"Dentists. An' that proves that we needn't have 'em really if savages don't need 'em. Savages have a jolly sight better time than us all round. They——"

"Now, William," said Mrs. Brown, hastily interposing before he had fully embarked upon this well-worn theme, "why not try to forget all about it till this afternoon? Things are hardly ever as bad as you think they're going to be."

William snorted again and went into the hall. There yet another thought struck him, and he returned to the dining-room.

"Why can't I have 'em all taken out an' get some false ones?"

"William *what* an idea!" said Mrs. Brown aghast.

"'S'a very good idea," said William earnestly. "Now jus' listen. It'd save you all the expense of me goin' to a dentist all the rest of my life. I bet false ones don't cost much. They'd cost less than all the dentist's bills till I'm grown up, anyway. I don't mind havin' cheap ones. I bet you can get cheap ones made out of the teeth of dead animals. I bet they sell 'em cheap at the Zoo, an places like that. I'd like to have wild animals' teeth. A tiger's or a leopard's, or somethin' like that. I'd rather have 'em than my own. An' he'd have to take 'em out with gas so I wouldn't feel it, an' I'd be all right for the rest of my life. An' it'd save you a lot of money."

"I never *heard* such nonsense, William," said Mrs. Brown. "Do stop talking and go out. Your appointment's at half-past two, you remember, and it's very kind of Ethel to give up her afternoon to taking you."

William was silent a moment, then, assuming his blandest expression, said: "I don't like to bother Ethel, Mother. S'pose I go alone, so's to save her the trouble."

"No, William," said Mrs. Brown firmly. "You know what happened the last time you went alone."

"Oh, *that* . . ." said William carelessly. "I'm a good bit older than that, now."

But he withdrew rather hastily, in order to avoid having to continue that particular topic. About a year ago he had gone alone to the dentist's, had tapped on the door so softly that he could hardly hear the sound himself, and immediately gone off to spend the afternoon with the Outlaws, reporting to his parents afterwards that he could get no answer to his knock.

He set off now, gloomily, to join the Outlaws, deciding not to return home till tea-time, when it would be too late for his appointment.

All the attempts of the Outlaws to cheer him were unsuccessful. He remained sunk in dejection.

"Gotter choose between bein' starved to death or torchered to death," he said. "That's a nice thing to happen in a country what's supposed to be civilised."

When lunch-time came, he found the pangs of hunger irresistible, and decided to go home for lunch, but slip away again quietly afterwards. He found, however, that this was impossible. His mother, indeed, seemed to be expecting him to make some such attempt (a lack of faith in him that grieved him deeply), and took possession of him the moment he had finished his lunch, in order to perform on him the process of cleansing and tidying that, in his eyes, added insult to injury.

"What does it matter what I *look* like?" he protested. "He's goin' to torcher me, not *look* at me. I don't see why anyone's gotter be *clean* to be torchered."

But Mrs. Brown brushed ruthlessly at his hair and made no answer.

Even then he had not quite given up hope of escape. There might yet be an interlude during which he would be supposed to be waiting for Ethel, which might easily be put to good use, but, to his disgust, he found Ethel ready in the hall when he came downstairs with Mrs. Brown. She wore her elder-sister air of aloofness and disdain that always irritated William. He decided not to expose to her any weakness that might conceivably form a handle against him later.

"I've been jolly well lookin' forward to this afternoon," he said breezily, as they set off. "I don't mind goin' to the dentist. I *like* goin' to the dentist. I'm not frightened of a bit of pain. . . ."

He continued in this strain till they reached Hadley. His jauntiness fell from him as they neared the dentist's gate, but he managed to enter with something of a flourish and even to produce an untuneful, devil-may-care whistle as he went up the walk to the front door.

"No, dentists don't worry me," he said. "I

always tell 'em: 'Go on, don't be afraid of hurtin'
me. I'm not afraid of a bit of pain.' I . . ."

His voice trailed away and he looked apprehensively
at the window of the surgery.

Ethel stood on the top step and pressed the bell.
William stood on the step just behind her. William's
attitude had reassured and disarmed her and she let
her thoughts wander off on their own sweet will. She
had had two hats sent on approval from a shop in
Hadley, and both of them suited her, and she couldn't
make up her mind which to have. She'd spent the
whole morning trying them on, one after the other.
One was the sophisticated type and the other the
unsophisticated type, and Ethel had never been able
to discover which type she really belonged to. She
was still pondering the question as she stood waiting
for the dentist's front door to open.

William took a furtive step backwards. She did
not notice. He took another, and another. Still
she did not notice. He found himself at the gate.
Ethel still stood on the top step, lost in the long, long
thoughts of youth. The gate stood open. Quick
as a flash of lightning, William vanished through it,
down the road, and round the nearest corner.

The dentist's receptionist, smart and trim in white
overall, opened the door. Ethel roused herself from
her dreams. (The sophisticated one, she thought,
on the whole. . . .)

"I've brought my young——" She turned to the
spot where William had been and stood gaping at it
in silent dismay. The earth had apparently opened
and swallowed him up.

*   *   *   *   *

William wandered slowly through the back streets of Hadley, keeping a wary eye open for Ethel, who might just conceivably, though not very probably, have set off in pursuit of him. He felt disillusioned with life in general. If he went home, his father would insist on another appointment being made with the dentist for to-morrow morning, and probably the dentist, thwarted of his prey one day, would set upon him with redoubled violence the next. Then there was Ethel. She would use the incident as a weapon against him, whenever she had need of one, which was very frequently. "Who ran away from the dentist?" she would say, with that nauseous sweetness that she used to point her jibes. It would be useless to explain that he had seen a friend in the distance, and, suddenly remembering that he had an important message for him, had run off in pursuit, and completely forgotten his appointment. Or that he had seen someone just about to be run over and had dashed off to rescue them. Suddenly, a stupendous thought struck him. Why go home at all? Why not set out to seek his fortune— a thing he'd been meaning to do for years, but had kept postponing to a more fitting occasion? What occasion could be more fitting than this? After all, one couldn't be worse off than at home, where one was washed and cleaned and dragged off to torturers without mercy. His mind went over the innumerable stories he had read about boys who set out to seek their fortunes. They were all reassuring. The heroes invariably returned to their native villages as million-aires and made handsome presents to all their old friends. Well, that ole dentist wouldn't get any present, he said to himself grimly. He'd be jolly lucky if he didn't get put in prison. And he'd never go to a dentist again all the rest of his life. That, at any rate, was a cheering prospect. He wondered how he'd stood it as long as he had. But he'd rather like to find a friend and companion, for the first stages of his journey—anyway, someone who was more used to the process of seeking his fortune than William was, and who would give him a few tips. One might waste a lot of time at first with not knowing just how to set about it. Walking along, deep in reverie, and not looking where he was going, he almost ran into a man coming from the opposite direction.

"An' where are you off to, young feller-me-lad, bargin' into folks like this?"

The man's voice was quite pleasant, despite the fact that William's bullet head had prodded his stomach with some force. William, as he apologised, studied him with interest. He had black hair and a rather dirty face, and he obviously belonged to the class of those who are seeking their fortune and have not yet found it. He looked, however, as if he knew the ropes of fortune-seeking and might be a considerable help to William, in the initial stages of it, at any rate. They might set out together. Perhaps they would find a fortune together, discover a diamond-mine or a hitherto undiscovered island, and come back joint millionaires.

"You'll know me next time you see me, won't you, younsgter?" went on the man, with a friendly grin.

As a matter of fact, there did seem to be something faintly familiar about the man's face, but William couldn't quite place it. It was possible, of course, that he'd seen him in the town before, but had not actually made his acquaintance till now.

"And where *are* you off to, in such a hurry?" went on the man.

He had a sympathetic manner, and William soon found himself pouring out the whole story.

"I thought p'raps you'd sort of help me," he ended. "I mean, I want to start workin' my way across the sea, same as most of 'em do, but I'm not sure how you get to it. The sea, I mean. I 'spect you sort of know how to get lifts to it, an' where to sleep an' how to get food, an' that sort of thing."

The man looked at him speculatively. He was known to his friends (and to the police) as Sandy Dick, but, having come out of prison only last week, and being of a modest, retiring disposition, he had darkened his naturally ginger hair, in order to escape notice as far as possible. And he recognised William. He had met William before. He had, in fact, on one notable occasion, prevailed upon William to hand over to him all his available cash. Obviously, however, William did not recognise him, for which he was thankful. For William seemed to him a direct gift from Providence. He was credulous and romantic. He was small and nimble. . . . Just before Sandy Dick had retired from public life, to take an enforced rest at the expense of his fellow citizens, he had made the acquaintance of a maid who worked in one of the houses on the outskirts of Hadley, and she had told him that her mistress belonged to that class so dear to the hearts of burglars, who conceal valuables in incongruous places and fondly hope that so they will escape detection.

This particular lady kept a valuable string of pearls

in a small box, wrapped in brown paper, addressed to James Limpsfield, Esquire, The Grange, Topham, on the blotter of her writing-table, as if just waiting to be posted. A burglar, she said confidently, would ransack the whole room and never look twice at the little brown paper packet addressed to James Limpsfield, on the writing-table. He had had to retire from public life before taking any definite steps in the matter, but immediately on his return, he had made his way back to the spot as unobtrusively as possible, in order to reconnoitre the position. To his disappointment he found that that particular maid had left, and that her successor was a grim elderly female who would, he was sure, be proof against all his blandishments. She had, however, gone out this afternoon, and her mistress had set off from the front gate soon afterwards. Between him and his goal (presuming that the brown paper packet was still on the writing-table) was only ten feet or so of piping, a sloping roof, and an open window. That would, in the ordinary way, have been nothing, but Sandy Dick had decided to pursue a policy of caution. He would only take a few seconds to swarm up the pipe, scale the roof and enter the window, but during those few seconds he would be in the full view of anyone who might happen to pass down the back street. That someone might be a policeman, and Sandy Dick had decided to give the blue-coated brotherhood a wide berth. He felt that he and they had had enough of each other's company for the present. He had been looking at the half-open window wistfully all the afternoon, had finally decided that it was not worth the risk, and had wandered off to another house in which he was interested. That, however, had proved to be disappointingly full of inhabitants and, before he had seriously begun his reconnoitring, a gardener had come out and indignantly ordered him off.

And then William had appeared. Sandy looked down at William almost affectionately, while he thought out his line of action. Finally he said: "Well, I *was* jus' goin' off to sea, myself."

"Can I come with you?" said William eagerly.

"Yes, but there's jus' one or two things I gotter do first," said Sandy Dick, "What's your name?"

"William Brown. What's yours?"

"James Limpsfield."

"Well, why can't we start at once? What've you gotter do first?"

"I'll tell you," said Sandy Dick, "if you'll just walk along with me a bit."

They set off, side by side, through the back streets of Hadley, towards the house that contained the magnetic brown paper packet.

"My father lives just near here," went on Sandy Dick, "but he's always been very cruel to me."

"Mine's the same," agreed William heartily. "Sendin' me off to be torchered! How'd *he* like it? *He* takes jolly good care to have false ones."

"And my step-mother's worse even than my father. They've cheated me out of all my money."

"I've never had any money," said William, "but I bet they'd have cheated me out of it all right, if I had."

"My father's turned me out of the house."

"Well, so has mine, in a way," said William, determined not to be outdone in hardship. "I mean, it comes to the same. . . . Come on. Let's start at once." He looked round anxiously as he spoke. He still had an uneasy suspicion that Ethel and the dentist might be searching the streets of Hadley for him. "Let's not stop here any longer."

Sandy Dick assumed an expression of stern virtue.

"There's one thing I must do first," he said. "My conscience won't let me go till I've done it. You see, my mother left a ring of hers for me that she wanted me to have, and my step-mother won't let me have it. It's there, made up in a parcel by my mother with my name on it, and the name of the house that ought to belong to me, and that they've cheated me out of. I don't mind about the house, but the ring's different. It's not that I want the ring for its own value, of course, because it's valueless. It's just that my mother wanted me to have it. It was her dying wish. And I can't go away with a clear conscience till I've got it."

"Why don't you tell the police about it?" said William.

Sandy Dick shivered involuntarily. "I shouldn't like to do that," he said. "I've got a kind heart. It's always been my curse, has my kind heart. I can't bear getting people into trouble. No, my idea is to go quietly into the house and take it. I feel that that's what my mother would like me to do. Then I can set off straight away to sea with you, with a clear conscience."

They had reached the back of the house now, and Sandy Dick gazed wistfully up at the pipe, the sloping roof, and the half-open window.

"It's on the writing-table in my step-mother's

bedroom, just across the landing from that room," he said. "Just to think that it's so near and I can't get it!"

"Why can't you go in an' get it?" said William.

"I'm afraid that if I met my father I'd kill him," said Sandy Dick.

"Well, I think that'd be a jolly good thing," said William simply.

"Well, of course, that's not the only reason," said Sandy Dick. "Another's that the doctors have told me that it's death to me to climb. Even to climb a few feet. I'm perfectly healthy in every other way, but it's death to me to climb."

A bright idea struck William. "I could easy nip up and get it," he suggested.

Sandy Dick heaved a secret sigh of relief, but shook his head as if unwilling to accept the offer.

"I don't want you to go into any danger for me," he said.

"Well, that's nothin'," said William. "I can nip in an' get it, 's easy 's easy. That's not the sort of danger I mind. It's bein' torchered I mind. Ordin'ry danger's nothin to me. . . ."

"Well . . ." said Sandy Dick, as if assenting reluctantly.

"Let's arrange some signals," said William, who liked to extract the utmost sensation from an adventure of this sort. "I'll whistle once from inside the house if there's danger for you, an' twice if I'm in danger an' want your help, an' you'll do the same from outside, will you?"

"Right you are!" agreed Sandy Dick.

William climbed over the fence, swarmed up the

pipe, scaled the sloping roof, and disappeared in at the half-open window. Sandy Dick remained below, poised for instant flight.

William found himself in a small bedroom, evidently of the spare variety—the bed dismantled; the dressing-table empty of toilet articles; the sole ornaments, family photographs that had obviously begun their career in the drawing-room twenty or thirty years ago. He opened the door and tiptoed across a landing into the bedroom opposite. It was empty, and—yes—there, upon a writing-table on a blotter was a small, brown paper packet addressed to "James Limpsfield, Esq.". It obviously contained the ring that had belonged to his new friend's mother, and that now belonged by rights to his new friend. He took it up and was just about to return by way of the spare bedroom, when another thought struck him. His heart was bursting with indignation at the dastardly fashion in which his new friend had been treated. Why shouldn't he get him something more useful than the valueless ring that was only needed to satisfy the demands of his conscience? He was very shabbily dressed, and from the top of the stairs William could see a thick, warm overcoat hanging from a hat-stand. It would help to keep poor James warm and dry on his journey to the coast. And it wasn't stealing. His cruel parents owed him that, at least, after cheating him out of his ring and house and all his money. It might even actually belong to James. It probably did. They'd probably pinched it as well as his house and his ring and his money. He went quietly down the staircase to the hall, and there—a horrible qualm of recognition crept over him. He knew this hall.

WILLIAM KNEW THIS PLACE. HE'D BEEN HERE BEFORE.

He'd been here before. He—— At that moment a door opened and the dentist came out.

"Tut, tut, tut!" he said irritably. "Glad you've had the sense to come at last. Silly, childish trick, running away like that. Made you half an hour late for your appointment. Fortunately, I've no other client this afternoon." He flung open the door

"GLAD YOU'VE HAD THE SENSE TO COME AT LAST," SAID
THE DENTIST.

of his surgery. "Come on in, and let's get to work."

With a feeling of sickening horror, William realised that his wanderings had brought him to the back of the very house from which he had fled. The shock had given a jolt to his memory, and he suddenly remembered where he had seen his new friend before. He wasn't called James Limpsfield. He was called Sandy Dick. Sandy Dick, who had robbed him of an enormous sum of money about a year ago. Sandy Dick, with hair mysteriously black instead of ginger, but Sandy Dick all the same.

In his surprise he dropped the packet. The dentist picked it up.

What on earth's the meaning of this?" he said mystified.

William inserted two fingers into the corners of his mouth and emitted a whistle that could have been heard not only in the next street, but in the next street but two. He waited for a few moments, till he was sure that Sandy Dick would have vanished from the landscape, then, with a sigh of resignation, he seated himself in the dentist's chair.

"I'll tell you all about it," he said, "if you'll promise not to use the drill."

CHAPTER IX

THE HOLEWOOD BEQUEST

WILLIAM did not know whether to be gratified or indignant when he heard that Aunt Louie had invited him to spend a week of the Easter holiday with her.

Aunt Louie herself was all right, of course, but she, in her turn, was staying with an aunt of her own—an ancient aunt, called Aunt Belle Holewood, whom William had never met. Aunt Louie had felt grateful to him ever since he had inadvertently provided her with the little wooden, carved figure which Aunt Belle had asked her to bring from South Africa, and which she had completely forgotten, and so Aunt Louie, who was still in England staying with Aunt Belle, had invited William, on the general principle that one good turn deserves another. She explained in her letter that Aunt Belle did not often leave her room, and that there would be a big garden for William to play in. There was also, she added, a dog, and a wood at the bottom of the garden. The dog and the wood and the element of the unknown in the situation, decided William. Aunt Louie he knew and liked. Aunt Belle, the house, the dog, the wood, were all unknown quantities, and the unknown always fascinated him. He agreed with that school of thought that holds that none of life's experience should be rejected.

Everything went smoothly enough at first. The house was large and not (as were some houses of his acquaintance), so overcrowded with knick-knacks that it was impossible to move without breaking something. The garden also was large, and did not (as did some gardens of his acquaintance), consist entirely of flowerbeds that must not be jumped over, and lawns that must not be trodden on. The private wood was a real wood and not (as were some private woods of his acquaintance) a narrow strip of trees, so closely planted with bulbs that games of Red Indians were impossible and that every movement brought shrieks of horror from the grown-ups. The dog was an overgrown Alsatian puppy called Thor, who had lived such a decorous life with Aunt Belle that he hardly realised that he *was* a puppy. Under William's guidance that omission was quickly rectified. Thor learnt to leap and gambol, to run after sticks and to burrow after rabbits. He seemed to know nothing about rats, either, and that deficiency William hastened to make good. He took him round to various farms and egged him on to every rat he could find. Thor proved an apt pupil, rising to a fine frenzy of excitement in pursuit, though he seldom actually caught his quarry. Even Aunt Belle turned out not to be the cantankerous, repressive old lady William had taken for granted she would be. She was a little absent-minded and distant in manner, it is true, but she did not appear to suffer from that rooted objection to any and every manifestation of youth that, in William's experience, was the chief characteristic of old age.

She was a dignified, grey-haired, little, old lady, and treated him with a formal courtesy that he found very impressive. Instead of telling him that he must be punctual for meals and never come into a room in muddy shoes, she offered him the freedom of the house and urged him to make himself completely at home.

"I wish your stay here to be a pleasant one, dear boy," she said, "and I hope that, if there is anything you want, you will not fail to ask for it. I shall not see much of you, as I spend my time chiefly in my room, but I have told everyone to do all they can to make you comfortable, and if there is anything I personally can do, you must not fail to let me know. I shall hope to see you from time to time."

William was deeply touched by this concern for his welfare. It was unlike anything that he had ever experienced at the hands of a grown-up in all his life before. The old lady, however, as she had said, spent most of her time upstairs, and her young guest saw nothing of her for the next few days. They passed happily enough. There were walks with Aunt Louie, who remained a congenial, understanding companion, games in the wood, and expeditions with Thor, in which Thor was initiated into his rightful kingdom of puppyhood. By the end of two days Thor quivered from nose to tail at the word "rats!" while the sight of one sent him into a state bordering on madness. He learnt, also, to stay and guard William's camp in the wood when William went in pursuit of (imaginary) hostile tribes or to accompany him on his reconnoitring expeditions, creeping silently through the bushes in his wake. William, in fact, had never come across any dog (except Jumble), who entered so heartily into the spirit of all his games, and picked up the general idea of them so quickly. Indoors, Aunt Louie provided books and games, and Aunt Belle's cook, meals that, both in quality and quantity, exceeded all William's previous experience. But, beneath the surface of this pleasant life, William soon detected an element of strain and anxiety. Aunt Louie would suddenly become silent and absent, frowning anxiously into space and not hearing what he said. She would go in to Aunt Belle's room for long and earnest talks, to come out looking worried and distrait.

A tall, important-looking man arrived and was closeted for a long time with Aunt Louie. Aunt Louie told William, when he had gone, that he was a solicitor. William was an adept at sensing when anything was afoot in the grown-up world, and he sensed it here almost at once. He didn't feel much curiosity, or even interest, however, as he knew that the grown-ups' attitude to life in general was wholly inexplicable. They worried about things that didn't seem worth worrying about and were pleased by things that seemed to William to contain small cause for rejoicing. He would not, therefore, have troubled himself with the mysterious undercurrent of grown-up emotion, had not Aunt Louie suddenly broken off a game of draughts on the last evening but one of his visit, to confide in him. At first he was rather annoyed because he was obviously winning, and he thought it a ruse on her part to avoid defeat, but he soon forgot all about the game in his interest in Aunt Louie's story.

"Poor Aunt Belle's very worried just now," she said with a sigh.

"Is she?" said William, crowning his latest king.

"OH, I'D UNDERSTAND IT ALL RIGHT," SAID WILLIAM. "I'D
HAVE WON IN ABOUT THREE MORE MOVES, WOULDN'T I?"

"Yes. It's about the bequest. The Holewood
bequest."

"What's that?" said William, and added: "It's
your turn."

But Aunt Louie only glanced absently at the draught-
board and sighed again.

"It's a very complicated story," she said. "I don't know if you'd understand it."

"Oh, I'd understand it all right," said William airily. "I'm jolly good at understanding things." He glanced wistfully at the board. "I'd have won in about three more moves, wouldn't I?"

"Yes, dear. . . . We'll count it that you've won." Honour being thus satisfied, William turned his attention to the matter in hand.

"All right," he said. "Well, now about this request thing——"

"Bequest, dear. It means a legacy. . . . Well, it began with Aunt Belle's father."

"Gosh!" said William, thinking of Aunt Bell's venerable figure. "As far back as that?"

"He was a colonel in the army."

"What did he fight in?" asked William with interest. "The Wars of the Roses? We've just started them at school."

"No, dear. Not quite as far back as that. Anyway, he was out in the East for some time, and he brought back with him a very beautiful carving of Kuan-yin dating from the end of the Ming dynasty."

"Oh, yes," said William helplessly.

"Kuan-yin is the Chinese Goddess of Mercy," explained Aunt Louie. "And the end of the Ming Dynasty was about the middle of the seventeenth century."

"Oh, yes," said William more helplessly still.

"Well, Colonel Holewood left it in his will to the town. He was a J.P. and a Councillor and all that sort of thing, and it was arranged that it was to be kept in the Free Library under a glass case, and it was always called the Holewood bequest."

William smothered a yawn. It was turning out to be the dullest story he'd ever heard. He'd much rather have finished the game of draughts. Or gone out for a run with Thor.

"But, when he died," went on Aunt Louie, "no one could find it. What probably happened was that it was stolen, because it was very valuable and everyone knew about the Holewood bequest. It was stolen, I am afraid, in the confusion of his last illness. He died very suddenly, and Aunt Belle was abroad at the time, and so there was a great deal of upset. Anyway, the thief, whoever it was, got away scot-free, and the town never had the Holewood bequest."

"An' is she still worryin' about it?" said William incredulously. "Well, I jolly well wouldn't worry about *that* if I was her."

"That's not the end of the story," said Aunt Louie. "She thought that she'd like to carry out the plan in her father's place, and leave a bequest to the town when she died."

"Jolly good idea!" agreed William. "So she got another of these Ying things from that Ming thing an'——"

"No, she couldn't do that," interrupted Aunt Louie. "The little statue was absolutely unique. There wasn't another like it in the world. But she's always been fond of travelling and of collecting, and she made a sort of museum of her travelling souvenirs and she wanted to bequeath that to the town as the Holewood bequest in place of the Kuan-yin."

"Jolly good idea!" said William again, thinking

that now she'd finished the not very interesting story he might suggest some more diverting occupation. But Aunt Louie's anxious expression did not lighten.

"I'm afraid it isn't, dear," she sighed. "You see— well, I'll show you her travel museum to-morrow morning, and I think you'll understand. You see, the loss of this little statue has always been a great grief to her and she's most anxious that there should be a Holewood bequest to the town, as her father meant there to be, and—well, to be frank, dear, she thinks that this travel museum of hers is much more interesting than it really is. It'll break her heart for there to be no Holewood bequest, but I'm afraid she'll have to face it."

"Why won't this travel museum do for one?" asked William.

Aunt Louie became still more confidential.

"I'm afraid they won't want it," she said, "and, really, I don't wonder. One can't tell her, of course, because, in a way, she spent her life making it, but it's of no value or interest at all to anyone in the world beside herself. She always meant it to take the place of the original Holewood bequest, and it will be a terrible shock to her to realise that they don't want it."

"Have they *said* they don't want it?" said William indignantly.

He liked Aunt Belle and thought that they ought to want anything she wanted them to want.

"Her solicitor's been instructed to offer it to them and they've sent back a message to say that they can't accept it. They've put it very nicely, of course, but that's what it comes to. We haven't dared to tell her yet. It isn't that she wants to glorify herself and her travels, you know, dear. She'd much rather that they had the original bequest—the loss of that's a great grief to her—but she does want her father's idea to be carried out in some form or another, and she's always thought that her travel museum would take its place."

"What's it like?" said William curiously. "Can I see it?"

"It's your bedtime now, isn't it?" said Aunt Louie, glancing at the clock. "I'll show it you first thing in the morning."

William went to bed and had a dream in which all his memories of museums in general tangled themselves gloriously together, and skeletons of prehistoric animals engaged in deadly combat with Egyptian mummies, watched by stone statues wearing the Crown Jewels, sitting astride Crimean War gun-carriages. The actual travel museum in the library, to which Aunt Louie conducted him after breakfast the next morning, proved a much tamer affair. It was, indeed, almost amazingly tame, though it covered a fair amount of space. On a table was ranged a large number of bottles, each containing water and each neatly labelled: "Water from the River Nile", "Water from the River Danube", "Water from the River Euphrates", etc. Aunt Belle's journeys had been extensive and few rivers of any importance were omitted. On a desk near was ranged a number of pebbles, such as one might pick up on any English beach. These, too, were neatly labelled: "Pebble from Adelaide", "Pebble from Beira", "Pebble from Malaga", "Pebble from San Francisco", etc. On yet another table were a large number of tram and bus tickets, each with its

appropriate label in Aunt Belle's copperplate hand.
"Tram ticket from Rome", "Tram ticket from
Moscow", "Tram ticket from Budapest", etc. Even
this was not all. There was a collection of pressed,
wild flowers—all of them flowers that grew quite
commonly in England—each of them neatly labelled:
"Celandine picked in the Forum", "Daisy found
growing on Acropolis", "Fern picked in Pompeii", etc.

Aunt Louie looked round helplessly.

"You see, dear," she said with a sigh, "it's full of
interest to her, of course, but it's of no intrinsic value
at all. I mean no public body could possibly accept
it. She can't understand that. She connects each
of them with her travels and adventures, and when
she sees them she sees the place they came from, and
all the interesting things there, and she can't understand that other people don't. To an ordinary person,
of course, they mean nothing at all. They're just—
they really are, I'm afraid—rubbish. There's a book
of snapshots, too, that's part of her collection, but
they're very poor. She doesn't see how poor they
are, of course. She sees the thing itself, not the snap-
shot of it. Well, I'm afraid that it's going to be a
dreadful shock to her when she knows that the town
has refused it."

"When will she know?" said William.

"She'll have to know to-day. The Town Clerk's
coming to tell her. It's—well, as I said before—it's
just that she wants there to be a Holewood bequest.
She's always been so distressed by the loss of that
statuette her father meant them to have."

"What time is this Town Clerk man coming?"
asked William.

"About four o'clock this afternoon, dear. But there's no need for you to worry over it. I only told you so that you'd understand why the old lady is just a little worried and absent-minded. . . . It's a lovely day, isn't it? You ought to be taking Thor for a run."

William went slowly out into the garden for Thor. Four o'clock. That gave him almost the whole day to ginger up the museum. He'd meant to spend his last day very differently, but he was determined that there should be a Holewood bequest, and he intended to spare no pains or effort to ensure it. Thor was disconcerted to find him so unusually sedate. William was thinking hard. The problem he'd set himself was a very difficult one, and the time in which he had to solve it was very short. Thor, who was an understanding sort of dog, followed quietly at his heels, waiting patiently till he should have time to attend to him and continue his education in puppyhood.

But William remained deep in thought. It was, except for one incident, a very uneventful walk, and even the one incident didn't seem particularly eventful at the time. A small, dejected-looking boy, standing in the doorway of a cottage, accosted William gloomily.

"Want a white rat?" he said.

"Course I do," replied William. "Anyone would. Why?"

"I've gotter get rid of mine. It's et up my mother's bedroom slippers, an' she's mad at me."

"Well . . ." William considered. "I dunno as my mother would want it if it eats bedroom slippers."

"It doesn't really," the boy assured him earnestly.

"It's all right, if you remember to feed it. That's what I told her," he continued aggrievedly. "I said: 'It's all right when I remember to feed it. It's only when I forget to feed it it starts on bedroom slippers an' things.' An' I promised I'd never forget again, but she wouldn't listen. Just as if a rotten ole pair of bedroom slippers mattered to anybody. They're jolly useful things, rats are. I told her so, but she wouldn't listen. It might give the alarm in case of fire, or somethin' like that. It'd serve her jolly well right if there was a fire an' we all got burnt up, with this rat not bein' there to give the alarm."

"How much d'you want for it?" enquired William in a businesslike tone.

"It's a jolly good rat," replied the boy. "I bet you'd have to give a lot for it in a proper animal shop. I bet I could have taught it tricks easy if I'd tried. An' it won't eat bedroom slippers if you remember to feed it. It was only hunger made it eat my mother's. I kept tellin' her so but she wouldn't listen. It's worth a jolly sight more, but I'll take a shilling."

"You can't," said William simply. "'Cause I've only got sixpence."

"All right," said the boy equally simply. "I'll take sixpence then. . . . I'll get it you now."

William looked down at Thor, who had been listening to the conversation with an interested air.

"I'd better not take it with *him* here," he said. "He's mad on rats. I've taught him to be. Look at him now," he went on proudly, for Thor, on hearing the word "rats", had pricked his ears again and stood quivering with eagerness. "If he saw even a tail of one, he'd go mad. So I'll have to keep it a secret

from him. But it'll be all right, 'cause I'm goin'
home to-morrow, so I'll come round for it this afternoon
without him, an' keep it in my bedroom till I go.
He's not allowed upstairs, so he won't know I've got
it."

"A'right," said the boy, "an' this rat's quite tame.
He'll stay in your pocket or anywhere. It was only
'cause he was hungry he et those bedroom slippers.
I said to her: 'You can't expect an animal to starve,
can you?' but she wouldn't listen. I expect he
thought her slippers were put there for him to eat.
He prob'ly et them out of politeness 'cause he thought
they'd been put there for him to eat. I told her that,
but she wouldn't listen. He must've had awful
stomache-ache after them. You'd think she'd be
sorry for him—wouldn't you?—'stead of bein' mad at
him. Anyway, if you bring your sixpence this afternoon, I'll have him all ready. He's called Wilfred
with the boy I got him from's father bein' a Fashist."

"All right," said William. "I'll come round for
him this afternoon," and set off again briskly down the
road with Thor at his heels.

Aunt Belle was to meet the Town Clerk in the
library at four o'clock and hear from him the news
of the rejection by the town of the Holewood bequest.
She had been partially prepared for the shock by Aunt
Louie, but she couldn't bring herself to believe it.

"The collection of a *lifetime*," she had said. "It's
absolutely unique. Of course, I know they'd rather
have had the Ming statuette. I'd rather myself that
they had it. But, surely, they won't *refuse* my
collection."

Aunt Louie had said that she was afraid they would,

and there the matter had rested. And now she had come down to see that the library was ready for the fateful interview. She walked in and threw an absent glance around—then stood, petrified by horror. For William had, in the meantime, gingered up the collection to the best of his ability. No longer did the bottles contain merely colourless river water. One had been filled with red ink and, beneath it was a notice in William's uneven handwriting: "Water from the Red Sea." One was a bright blue and beneath it William (with vague memories of popular songs), had written: "Water from the Danube." Another was filled with black ink and had the label: "Water from the Black Sea." In another there floated a selection of dead insects and several dead minnows. This was labelled: "Water from the Dead Sea." The collection of pressed flowers had been swept away and in its place stood an extraordinary array of botanical specimens brought in from the garden and freely adapted by William. There was a tulip with a daffodil's head wired on just below the tulip's head, there were primroses painted green and black, there was a fern decorated with gold and silver paint, grape hyacinths grew, surprisingly, from an apple-tree branch, and curious blooms formed of multi-coloured plasticene alternated with yellow azaleas on a hawthorn twig. Each of these horticultural phenomena bore an appropriate (if erratically spelt) label: "Flower from Sellon", "Flower from Veeenner", "Flower from Parris", etc.

The pebbles, too, had been swept away and in their place were strange strips of clay, painted bright colours. As Aunt Louie stood there, petrified with horror, William entered, smiling complacently. He had just been round to collect Wilfred, who was now reposing peacefully in his coat pocket. He was, as the boy had said, a very tame rat, and seemed quite content to stay in William's pocket, nibbling at his handkerchief.

"Well, they jolly well ought to take it now, oughtn't they?" he said proudly. "I took a jolly lot of trouble over it, an'——"

At this point Aunt Belle entered, and as she looked round there came an expression into her face, beside which Aunt Louie's horror paled into nothingness.

"My museum!" she cried wildly. "My collection! . . . The Holewood bequest! . . . *Ruined!*"

She was, obviously, going to say a good deal more when the housemaid opened the door, to admit a large, sleek man who was evidently the Town Clerk. He didn't even glance at the collection. He had already seen it and weighed it in the balance and found it very definitely wanting.

"I'm sorry to be the bearer of an unfavourable decision, Miss Holewood," he began pompously, but at that moment there came yet another interruption. For Thor entered the library and, just as Thor entered it, Wilfred happened to poke his head out of William's pocket to see what was going on. Immediately all was confusion. Wilfred leapt on to the floor, then over the tables and desk. Thor hurled his great body in pursuit, barking loudly. William hurled himself after Thor in a futile attempt to restrain him. The collection was scattered right and left— the bottles upset and plants dismembered. The Town Clerk joined in the fray, entangling himself

H

in William and Thor and rolling over on to the hearthrug, bringing William with him. William, in a
desperate attempt to save himself, clutched at a half-
open drawer in the desk on the left. The drawer
came out with a sound of wrenching wood, and there,

THE TOWN CLERK ROLLED OVER ON TO THE HEARTHRUG
BRINGING WILLIAM WITH HIM. WILLIAM CLUTCHED AT A
HALF-OPEN DRAWER.

AUNT LOUIE SCREAMED.

from a secret compartment that formed a false back
to the drawer, rolled out a little ivory statuette.

"The thing!" screamed Aunt Louie.

"The Kuan-yin!" cried Aunt Belle.

"The Holewood bequest," said the Town Clerk reverently, as he disentangled himself from William and resumed his official dignity.

They stood round it, beaming with rapture. All except William. William wasn't interested. He'd taken a lot of trouble gingering up the collection, and it had all been spoilt. He washed his hands of the whole concern. Rescuing Wilfred from the top of the bookcase, and keeping him well out of the way of Thor (who was somewhat chastened by the full impact of the Town Clerk's massive form), he set off to the kitchen to find him something to eat. . . .

CHAPTER X

WILLIAM AND THE OLD MAN IN THE FOG

WILLIAM wandered disconsolately about the crowded village hall looking, without much interest, at the various stalls, each laden with the useless articles that are characteristic of that peculiarly English institution, the Sale of Work. He had been allowed to come as a treat and had taken for granted that some form of diversion would present itself, but, so far, his hopes had been disappointed. None of his friends seemed to be there, and the only people who had taken any notice of him had been elderly ladies raffling tea-cosies, and even they had lost interest in him as soon as they found that he wasn't going to buy a ticket. His mother had given him sixpence to spend and he had bought a packet of sweets at the home-made sweet stall, which had turned out to be so burnt that even he could not eat them. He had taken them back and indignantly demanded his sixpence, but the lady in charge (who happened to have made the sweets in question) had coldly reminded him that it was "all for the Cause", and had refused either to exchange the sweets, or to give him back the sixpence. The knowledge that the "Cause" was the repairing of the churchyard wall (whose present dilapidated condition made it an excellent playground) did little to mitigate his annoyance.

He had wandered past the fancy stall, the household stall, the toilet stall, the cake stall (that delayed him a little, but the stallholder, catching him in the act of filching a currant from the top of a currant bun—its only currant, moreover—indgnantly ordered him off), and was just on the point of leaving the hall in disgust, when he caught sight of a screen with a notice "Fortune Teller" pinned on to it. It was a small, unimportant-looking screen, tucked away in a small, unimportant-looking corner, and a small, unimportant-looking woman sat nervously at a table inside.

She wasn't a very good fortune teller and knew that she wasn't a very good fortune teller and wouldn't have come if they could have got anyone else. She'd only had two clients so far, and had been very unsuccessful with both. The last one, an elderly spinster, had gone off in a state of high dudgeon after being informed that she had four children, and had refused to pay her half-crown. The fortune teller was beginning to suspect that it wasn't one of her Days. There were Days when she Could, and Days when she Couldn't, and this was, quite evidently, one of the Days when she Couldn't.

In any case, she'd only taken up the subject a fortnight ago, and it was turning out to be much more difficult than she'd thought it would be. She saw William's head poked inquisitively round the edge of the screen and brightened. A boy. Surely a boy would be easy enough.

"Come in, my dear," she said. "It's two and six for a full reading."

The rest of William followed his head.

"I've not got two and six," he said gloomily. "I've not got anything. I only had sixpence, an it's been stole off me. Well, I call it stealin', anyway. A dog couldn't 've et 'em.'' He handed her the paper bag. "Try if you can.''

The fortune teller nervously refused.

"I don't mind anythin' a *bit* burnt,'' went on William expansively, "an' I bet there's not many things I can't eat. If there's a tiny bit of the real taste left through the burnt I can eat it, but these don't taste of anythin' but burnt. Not *anythin'*. I bet she *made* 'em of burnt. An' when you think what you could get for sixpence! Sixpence! . . . Well, I'm jolly well not comin' to one of these things again, not if they go down on their bended knees to ask me to. I'd like to see her eat 'em herself. Said there was real butter in 'em. Real burnt in 'em, she meant.''

The fortune teller looked at him speculatively. He was garrulous and ingenuous, and he was presumably acquainted with most of the local inhabitants. He was the type to know and be known wherever he was. He might prove useful. She cast her eye round the room for possible clients.

"Who's that pretty girl over there?'' she said.

William's gloom deepened.

"Her?'' he said with an expression of disgust. "Call *her* pretty? She's my sister, an' a jolly rotten sister she is, too. Wouldn't even give me a penny. Not a *penny*. I said: 'Well, try'n' eat 'em yourself an' see how *you* like 'em. I bet I ought to be *paid* sixpence for jus' tastin' 'em.' I said: 'If it was you, I'd give you somethin' to make up. I'd give you another sixpence, or buy you some more sweets,' but she wouldn't take any notice. An' she's got heaps of money. She's always buyin' things. I bet she'll

"WHO IS THAT PRETTY GIRL OVER THERE?" ASKED
THE FORTUNE TELLER.

come along here in a minute to have her fortune told.
She's always havin' her fortune told. I'd jolly well
like *her* to have to live on burnt for a day or two, an'
see how *she* likes it."

The fortune teller looked at Ethel again.   She was

"CALL *HER* PRETTY?" SAID WILLIAM WITH DISGUST.
"SHE'S ONLY MY SISTER."

quite the most attractive girl in the room. If she
had her fortune told, and was pleased by it, probably
everyone else would follow suit. She sympathised
with William over the burnt sweets and began to chat
with him in a pleasant, desultory fashion. William,

touched by her sympathy and interest, prattled volubly about his family and family affairs. By the time that Ethel had decided to have her fortune told and, surrounded by a giggling bodyguard, had begun to make her way across the room to the screen, the fortune teller felt that she knew all about her that it was possible to know.

" *Said* she'd come," muttered William bitterly. "Doesn't mind spendin' money on fortune tellers an' suchlike, but won't spend a penny to save her own brother from bein' poisoned to death. I only had a bit, an' I can still taste it. I think it's gettin' worse. It's prob'ly spreadin'. Serve her right if I died of it."

Enlarging upon this theme, he delayed his departure till Ethel was actually at the entrance. The fortune teller was anxious that they should not meet. The girl would be much less impressed by her powers if she knew that she had just been talking to her young brother.

" Go out at the back," she whispered to William, and pushed him out at the back of the screen, where it joined the wall. William began to scrape his way out between the screen and the wall, when it suddenly occurred to him to stop just out of sight and listen to Ethel's fortune. It might be interesting and; anyway, he'd nothing else to do.

He listened with growing amazement. Why, every single thing the fortune teller said was true. She even told her that she'd sprained her thumb last week at Squash Rackets, and that she'd been to a dance on Saturday. She described her various admirers and her attitude to each. She told her that she was going away to-morrow on a fortnight's visit to some friends in the North.

All this sounded so important and portentous, brought out in the fortune teller's most fortune-telling voice, that William did not recognise it as part of his inconsequential chatter of a few minutes ago, and was fully as impressed as Ethel herself.

"Gosh!" he kept saying to himself in amazement. "That's abs'lutely true. Abs'lutely."

Ethel, on the other side of the screen, kept up a running commentary of surprise and admiration.

"But, how marvellous! . . . That's wonderful. . . . Yes, I *am* going away to-morrow. . . . Fancy it being marked on my hand like that. . . . I think you're simply marvellous. . . ."

William watched her pay her half-crown and go out to join her giggling bodyguard.

"She's simply wonderful," she said. "She told me . . ." She lowered her voice to a whisper, and the bodyguard crowded eagerly round.

William was just going to abandon his somewhat uncomfortable position when he saw that Robert had now entered the screeened-off partition, and was sitting down at the table opposite the fortune teller. He decided to stay at his post a little longer and learn what was going to happen to Robert. Ethel's fortune had been so convincing that it would be interesting to hear Robert's.

The fortune teller began to ply Robert with artless questions, but Robert was determined to give nothing away, and answered in monosyllables. The fortune teller sighed and bent over his hand.

"There's a legacy coming to you soon," she said. (A legacy was always fairly safe. No one could say it was quite impossible, anyway.) "Yes, a legacy. I see it plainly. A legacy. Have you any relative who's likely to leave you a legacy?"

"No," said Robert.

"Perhaps it's someone you've befriended."

"I've never befriended anyone," said Robert uncompromisingly.

"Perhaps not knowingly," said the fortune teller, who was beginning to dislike him intensely, "but you may have befriended someone without realising it, out of sheer kindness of heart. It may not even be any-one you know. Some little kindness done by the way. I once knew a boy who helped an old man who was lost in the fog, and the old man left him all his fortune. . . . As for your character" she went on hastily, seeing that Robert was opening his mouth to deny indignantly that he had ever helped any old man anywhere, "you're sensitive and highly strung."

She proceeded to describe Robert's character at great length, and William, who wasn't interested in Robert's character, stole softly away.

Though not interested in Robert's character, he was intensely interested in Robert's legacy. He believed in it implicitly. Had not the fortune teller correctly described the accident to Ethel's thumb and prophesied her visit to the North to-morrow? It followed, there-fore, irrefutably that Robert would soon be the possessor of a vast fortune left to him by an old man whom he had once helped in a fog. . . .

William had no intention of spreading this news, but he couldn't resist dropping a few hints here and there.

"Wait till Robert comes into his money," he said to Miss Bellfield when she deplored the unsatisfactory financial state of the Providence Club, over which she presided. "I bet he'll help you out."

Miss Bellfield gazed at him in astonishment.

"What money?" she asked.

"Oh, this leg'cy of his," replied William airily.

"What legacy?" persisted Miss Bellfield.

"This leg'cy this ole man's leavin' him."

"What old man?" said Miss Bellfield, who never let anything go once she'd got hold of it.

"Well," explained William somewhat reluctantly. "I don't know as he wants people to know, but he helped this ole man in a fog once, an' this ole man's leavin' him all his money."

"How does he know he is?"

"He told him. This ole man told him."

Miss Bellfield sighed, remembering bitterly a certain great-aunt of her own.

"People often say that, my dear boy, and forget to make a will."

"Oh, he's made his will," said William airily. "He's made his will all right. An' it's all comin' to Robert. Every penny of it."

Again Miss Bellfield sighed, remembering this time an uncle on her mother's side.

"Those are the people," she said darkly, "who go on living and living and living."

"He won't," said William. "He's dyin' now."

"How do you know?"

"They've sent word. He can't possibly live more'n a week or two, now."

"They've actually told Robert that he's the heir?"

"Yes."

"Dear me! How interesting!" said Miss Bellfield.

William was feeling a little uneasy. The main fact of the legacy, of course, was true enough (hadn't the fortune teller said so in so many words?), but he was aware that, carried away by his imagination, he had added a few details that did not strictly conform to fact.

"Don't say anythin' to Robert about it," he said anxiously.

"But why not, dear?" smiled Miss Bellfield.

"He said he didn't want people to mention it to him," said William. "He said so most particular."

"Yes, dear. I do understand," sighed Miss Bellfield. "It's like counting your chickens before they're hatched. Like waiting for dead men's shoes. I think it shows great delicacy of feeling in Robert, and I, for one, will respect it."

"P'raps I oughtn't to've told you," said William, his apprehension growing as he remembered one or two of his wilder flights of fancy. "P'raps you'd better not tell anyone else."

"Of course I won't, dear boy," said Miss Bellfield. "I'll keep the little secret most faithfully."

She quite honestly meant to keep the little secret most faithfully, but like William, she couldn't resist dropping a hint here and there, and by evening the whole village knew that Robert had been left an enormous fortune by an old man whom he had once helped in a fog, that the old man was lying on the point of death, and that his lawyer had formally notified Robert that he was the sole heir. In order to salve her conscience, she always added that Robert, out of delicacy of feeling, was anxious that no one should mention the subject to him.

('After all," she said to herself, "it doesn't matter
their *knowing* if they don't *say* anything.")

The village was agog with excitement. Wherever
Robert appeared he was treated with respect and
deference. Old friends hastened to renew the bonds
of friendship. New friends anxiously consolidated
their position. Robert, as the future disposer of
millions (the fortune had increased by leaps and bounds
as it was handed on from mouth to mouth), was invested with a new glamour. People who had thought
him dull and ordinary, thought him dull and ordinary
no more. Girls who had publicly announced that they
wouldn't marry Robert Brown if he was the last man
in the world, hastily revised their views on the subject.
But—partly because of Robert's wishes (which had
always been conscientiously tacked on to the report),
and partly because no one wished their suddenly
increased friendliness to be put down to interested
motives—the legacy, though occasionally hinted at,
was never actually mentioned to him.

Mrs. Brown had been summoned to the sick bed of a
sister, and Ethel had gone North on the prophesied
visit, or they might, of course, have put an end to the
misunderstanding. As it was, Robert remained the
fêted, courted idol of the neighbourhood. Robert, of
course, could not fail to notice the changed attitude of
everyone around him, but it did not surprise him. For
Robert had secretly purchased a book, which he had
seen advertised in a magazine, called: "How to be
Popular." The advertisement was illustrated by the
picture of a tall, handsome, young man in the centre of a
crowd of admiring youths and maidens, who clustered
about him, fixing on him adoring eyes and obviously

hanging on his slightest word. It was that picture
that had inspired Robert to send for the book. ("Plain
wrapper. One and six, post free.") It was so unlike
his own experience when he appeared in public. . . .
There was a typewritten letter with the book, which
said: "After reading this book and carrying out these
simple rules, your whole life will be changed."

Robert had at once set to work to study the book in
the seclusion of his bedroom. It told him, in a short,
pungent preface, that he possessed secret powers of magnetism and attraction that only needed to be liberated.
It told him that his diffidence and self-distrust was the
effect of conflicting forces that only needed to be harm-
onised. It told him that, in spite of any evidence to the
contrary, he was possessed of a dominating, irresistible,
dynamic personality. It hinted that, when the opposite
sex should see him as he really was (dominating, irresistible, dynamic), it would fall for him in shoals. Robert
didn't particularly want it to fall for him in shoals
(though the prospect was not without its attractive
side), but he did want Peggy Barlow to fall for him.

He'd been on and off with Peggy Barlow for years
and now he was quite definitely on, though Peggy,
on her side, was quite definitely off. She had told him
only the other afternoon that she was sick of the sight
of him and never wanted to see him again.

That had increased his wavering devotion to fever
pitch, and it was chiefly on Peggy's account that he had
risked the large sum of one and six on "How to be
Popular". He studied the simple rules with frowning
concentration. They were, indeed, so simple that,
though he was going to give them a good trial, he hadn't
really very much hope of success.

The rule that came over and over again was: "Hold up your Head and Look the World in the Face." Then followed a lot of little sentences that you had to say to yourself as you Looked the World in the Face, such as: "There is nothing I cannot do." (Robert, who was an essentially truthful boy, shrank somewhat from this palpable untruth, but determined to go the whole hog and say it with the rest.) "I can if I will, not I will if I can." "Nothing and no one can withstand me." "Inexhaustible power surges within me." "Health and happiness are mine," and several others of like trend. Robert conscientiously committed these slogans to memory and sallied forth the next morning to Look the World in the Face.

He was amazed by the instant success of the system. (It happened to be the day that the news of his legacy had spread through the village.) Everyone he spoke to (saying the little slogans to himself the while) gave him a new and respectful attention. People he didn't speak to came and spoke to him with a friendliness, an obvious admiration, that no one had ever accorded him before.

The extent to which his secret powers of magnetism and attraction were being liberated, amazed him. The rules of "How to be Popular" worked like magic. What a pity he hadn't bought it years ago! How strange that everyone didn't buy it! (It occurred to him to wonder what would happen if they did, though, because if everyone was dominating and attractive there'd be no one left to be dominated and attracted, and a most awkward situation would arise.)

Still, there was no doubt that he possessed, as the book had told him he did, an irresistible personality. Certainly, now that it was liberated no one seemed able to resist it. Peggy came down to the gate to meet him as he approached her house and, with a sweetness that made her almost unrecognisable, suggested a walk in the woods. During the walk she discoursed upon her utter indifference to wealth and luxury, and told him at least eleven times that she always liked people for themselves alone—a choice of subjects that Robert would have found rather strange if he had not been so busy saying his little slogans to himself that he hardly listened. And it wasn't only Peggy. Clarinda Bellew, Dolly Clavis, Emmeline Moston, Cornelia Gerrard, Dorita Merton—girls who'd had no use for him at all for years—suddenly seemed to fall under the spell of his liberated powers of attraction, his new dynamic personality. There was no doubt at all that he was Born to Succeed, as the little book had said he was. And it wasn't only young people. Older people in the village, too, seemed suddenly to succumb to his fatal magnetism. Miss Milton, for one, waylaid him as he was passing her gate and accosted him with tender enquiries about his health.

"I'm quite well, thank you," said Robert somewhat absent-mindedly, as he silently repeated: "I can if I will, not I will if I can."

Miss Milton looked at him fondly. "Your health is very precious, dear boy."

Robert smiled sheepishly, and told himself that there was Nothing he Couldn't Do.

"You know, dear boy," continued Miss Milton, sinking her voice confidentially, "the possession of wealth is a great responsibility."

Robert agreed absently and assured himself that Inexhaustible Power Surged within him.

"It's so important," said Miss Milton, "that it should be used for the public good and not for private pleasure."

Robert agreed, remembering suddenly to Hold up his Head and Look the World in the Face. Miss Milton, a little startled by the sudden glare he turned on her, continued:

"My little Society for Providing Comforts for Sick Pets is sadly in need of funds. You won't forget that, will you?"

Robert said vaguely that he wouldn't, and went on assuring himself once again that there was Nothing he Couldn't Do.

It occurred to him that most people who spoke to him nowadays seemed to want to discuss the possibilities and responsibilities of wealth with him. The Vicar had stopped him one day and talked to him at length about the choir's crying need of new surplices. A friend of his father's, who had never spoken to him before had accosted him and held forth about a mine in South America that only wanted a little capital to secure at least fifty per cent for its shareholders. Peggy Barlow, though repeating at regular intervals that money meant nothing to her, kept telling him how much she had always longed for a diamond brooch, a real pearl necklace and a high-powered motor-car.

The only explanation he could think of was that, now that his dynamic personality was released, people naturally wished to discuss more serious subjects with him than the weather and football results. He was quite willing to let people choose their own subjects of discussion, because the silent repetition of his little slogans, which had proved so astoundingly successful, took most of his attention.

Meantime, William had been somewhat disconcerted by the result of his disclosure of the fortune teller's prophecy. He still believed implicitly in the actual legacy, but he was aware that he had added to the bare fact a little more embroidery than was strictly justified. Moreover, he continued to add it. Though scrupulous not to mention the subject to Robert, people bombarded William with questions, and William, who never liked to admit himself at a loss, answered them all. He described in detail the incident of the old man's being found by Robert, wandering lost in the fog. He described the old man's home, his appearance, his family, his disposition. He said that he lived near the aunt whom Robert had been to visit in the summer, and that the incident had occurred during his visit. That made the fog a little puzzling, but when someone suggested a sea mist William eagerly accepted the explanation. He said that the old man had quarrelled with all his family because they made such a fuss about him keeping white rats and minnows in his bedroom—a reason which seemed to William a perfectly convincing one, but which his interlocutors found somewhat puzzling. The whole story, indeed, as told by William, had a somewhat exotic air, but it never occurred to anyone to doubt it. William's accounts of things were always confused, but he was not likely to have invented the main fact of the legacy. They continued to regard Robert with excited interest. And so Robert, delighted but just a little bewildered, was swept along by the full, strong stream of popularity. His popularity, indeed, was almost embarrassing. The young man in the advertisement was ostracised in comparison. People

asked his advice about all sorts of things. He had so
many engagements that he had to buy a little book and
put them down. And he continued to Hold up his
Head and Look the World in the Face and repeat the
little slogans to which he thought he owed everything.

The fact that, at the end of the week, he won three
pounds in a football pool, seemed to him only a natural
part of this triumphant career. To William it was
the fulfilment of the prophecy. Three pounds was,
to him, untold wealth. Thousands and millions were
vague terms used to express three pounds or there-
abouts. And the word "legacy", too, was probably
a loose term, used to express money coming un-
expectedly from any quarter. Anyway, he was glad
that it had come at last. He was sick of being asked
questions about it and having to make up answers.
He was relieved to be freed from the necessity of
reconciling conflicting statements and trying to remember what he had last said about the old man's
habits, appearance, and family. He walked through
the village wearing an air of importance.

"Robert's got that money I told you about," he
told everyone. "It came this morning."

The news spread like wildfire. Robert's legacy had
arrived. They recalled William's wilder statements,
though the more cautious prudently discounted them.

"I hardly think it's actually millions, but it's
probably thousands."

Robert, going into the village for some cigarettes,
was amazed at his reception—or, at least, he would
have been amazed if his new popularity hadn't accustomed him to that sort of reception. People accosted
him on all sides, and wrung him by the hand.

"Congratulations, old boy. . . . *Heartiest* congratulations."

Some of them hailed him facetiously as "Lord
Nuffield". He supposed that William had told
everyone about his three pounds. Trust that little
beggar to spread any news there was to spread! Still,
Robert was not sorry that everyone should know of
his success. It marked him out as the sort of person
who couldn't fail at anything, even at a football
pool. When they asked him what he was going to do
with it, and he said he was going to buy new tyres for
his motor-cycle, they thought he was being funny and
roared with laughter. On the other hand, when they
asked him for donations to the Cricket Club, the
Football Club, the Village Hall Fund, and the Choir
Treat, he thought they were being funny and roared
with laughter in his turn.

A few of the more honest ones said that he was
behaving very queerly about his fortune. Others said
it was all part of his charm—that charm that he had
so recently acquired.

By evening, Robert had completely disposed of the
three pounds. He had bought a pair of quite good
tyres for his motor-cycle, given a shilling to William,
and spent the remaining five shillings on a present for
Peggy. It was, he considered, an extremely handsome
present—a large, paste brooch in the shape of a motor-
car. The shopman had said they were a special line
and could never be repeated at that price. The Mercers
were giving a fancy-dress party that night, and he
meant to present it to her then. He looked forward
with pleasant anticipation to her gratitude. She was
grateful for anything and nothing nowadays. Strange

"HOW ON EARTH DO YOU THINK I COULD BUY REAL
DIAMONDS?" GASPED ROBERT.

to remember how aloof and disdainful she had been
only a short time ago.   His liberated dynamic personality had made a completely different person of her.

He was wearing his "School for Scandal" costume
and had taken a good deal of trouble burnishing it up
and trying to take out the stain where someone had
spilt claret-cup on it the last time he'd worn it.   His
efforts had only spread the stain, but he wasn't worrying
because his new popularity would carry off any amount

of claret-cup stains. William was going in his Red
Indian suit. The two set out together, Robert silent
and aloof. He had not thought it worth while to
book many dances beforehand, as every girl he knew
had hinted that she was keeping every dance free for
him. "I can if I will," he murmured to himself as
he went along. "Nothing and no one can withstand
me." ... "Inexhaustible power surges within me." ...
William, on his side, was feeling at peace with himself
and all the world. There would be jellies, blanc-
manges and trifles, and no one to restrain him, for
Robert would be busy with his own affairs. Moreover,
Robert had come into his money and so that episode
was satisfactorily closed. People would have to stop
asking him questions about it. He was sick to death
of that old man in the fog. . . . Robert had given
him a shilling and he still had sixpence left. Life,
therefore, was very rosy for William, and he was
grateful to the fortune teller, who, he felt, was the
originator of this state of things.

Peggy Barlow was waiting for Robert just inside the
dance-room. Clarinda Bellew, Dolly Clavis, Emmeline
Moston, Dorita Merton and Cornelia Gerrard were
waiting for him, too, but Peggy got in first. Robert
took her to an alcove and pressed the little packet into
her hands.

"Just a small present," he explained modestly.

Peggy opened it and drew a deep breath of delight.
"Oh, Robert!" she gasped. "*Diamonds!*"

Robert laughed.

"Well, hardly *diamonds* exactly," he said, "but
they do get them up awfully well, nowadays, don't
they?"

Peggy stared at him.

"Do you mean they aren't *real?*" she said indignantly.

Robert's mouth dropped open.

"How on *earth* do you think I could buy real diamonds?" he gasped.

"You got your money this morning, didn't you?"

"Yes," said Robert, "but——"

She interrupted him angrily.

"And you bring me a cheap thing like this!"

"Hang it all!" expostulated Robert. "It cost five shillings. I don't call *that* cheap."

"Five *shillings!*" echoed Peggy hysterically. "Five *shillings!* You got all that money this morning, and you spend five shillings on me."

"It was a jolly sight more than I could afford, too," said Robert resentfully.

"You're going to be very careful of it, aren't you?" sneered Peggy.

"I don't know what you call careful," said Robert. "I've spent it all, anyway."

She stared at him in incredulous horror.

"Spent all *that?*" she said. "You must be mad."

"It was only three pounds," said Robert.

"Three——?" Words failed her.

"Yes. Three pounds from one of those football pools. I've been trying for months."

"But what about your legacy?" she said.

"Legacy?" said Robert wildly. "What legacy?"

"The legacy from the old man in the fog."

"The——" Robert's head reeled. "The *what?*"

"The old man in the fog. The one you found lost and showed the way to, and who left you his fortune."

Robert's face was a mask of bewilderment.

"I don't know what you're talking about," he said. "You must be thinking of someone else."

Peggy stamped angrily.

"Of *course*, I'm not thinking of anyone else. . . . You spread this story just to get me to take some notice of you—though, as I said all along," she interpolated hastily, "money means less than nothing to me—and then you have the nerve to stand there and tell me that it was all a lie. A deliberate lie!"

Robert felt that he must be dreaming.

"Listen!" he pleaded. "I never told you about any old man in a fog. . . ."

"No," agreed Peggy contemptuously, "you were too much of a skunk even to do that. You got someone else to do your dirty work. You spread the story through an innocent child. *Oh!*" She gave an exaggerated shudder of disgust. "I didn't think that such a *worm* could exist. I shall never speak to you again as long as I live, and neither will any other decent girl."

With that she turned on her heel and left him. He stared after her, more bewildered than ever. He'd never heard such rubbish in his life. She'd gone mad. She must have gone mad. Well, he didn't care. And he'd just show her, too. Clarinda Bellew, Dolly Clavis, Emmeline Moston, Dorita Merton and Cornelia Gerrard had been pestering him for dances all the week. He approached Clarinda and asked her condescendingly for a dance. But already the report was flying round the room. Robert Brown hadn't got any legacy, after all. He'd only won three pounds in a football pool and, what was more, already spent it. Immediately Robert became the ordinary, rather stupid youth he had been before the legend of his wealth had invested him with glamour. Clarinda looked at him disdainfully and said that her programme was full, without even trying to hide from him the fact that it wasn't. Dazedly, he passed on to Dolly Clavis. Dolly Clavis didn't even bother to speak to him. She merely looked him up and down, then turned on her heel and left him.

Robert struggled to collect his forces. . . . This was a crisis. He'd forgotten to say the little slogans since he entered the dance hall and this was the result. He stood quite still and said them over to himself, then grimly controlled and self-possessed, approached Honoria Mercer.

"Have you a dance for me, Honoria?" (I can if I will. I can if I will. Nothing and no one can withstand me. Nothing and no one can withstand me. Inexhaustible power surges within me. Inexhaustible power surges within me.)

Honoria gave a nasty, sarcastic laugh and, copying Dolly Clavis, turned on her heel and left him. (She flattered herself that she had a much better heel-turn than Dolly's.)

Then Robert faced final failure. The slogans had ceased to work. It wasn't any use repeating them any more because they seemed now to have the opposite effect to the one they had had at first. They were turning people definitely against him. Evidently they only acted for a certain time, and then the liberated personality returned to prison, and the magnetism ceased to function. There was certainly nothing dynamic about him now. He sat staring gloomily in front of him, while people passed him haughtily, contemptuously, with averted faces, or stood in clusters, obviously discussing him, referring to his Looking the World in the Face as an "imbecile stare". There was no getting away from the fact that the slogans had failed. But, surely, there was more than that to it. What had Peggy said about an old man in a fog? What had she said about an innocent child? He'd taken them for meaningless ravings, but it occurred to him suddenly that there must be something behind them, and that he must get to the bottom of things. William was generally at the bottom of things, but he couldn't be at the bottom of this, because he didn't come into it at all. Or did he? There was something ominous in the phrase, "innocent child". The more he thought of it the more certain he was that William *was* at the bottom of it. He'd go to him at once and drag the truth out of him.

He looked round the room. William was nowhere to be seen, but Robert knew where he'd be. With firm and measured tread, with the light of vengeance gleaming in his eye, he set off in the direction of the supper-room. . . .